SWORDS FOR HIRE

Two of the most unlikely
heroes you'll ever meet

by Will Allen

CenterPunch Press
Cincinnati

Swords For Hire
Two of the most unlikely heroes you'll ever meet

A novel by Will Allen

Copyright © 2003 Paul M. Allen and Anne Allen Strand
Edited by Paul M. Allen
Cover painting and book illustrations by David Michael Beck
Cover design by Bob Dilgard
Foreword by Nancy Cartwright

This book is a work of fiction. Names, places, and characters, especially the guy with the worms, are the product of the author's imagination. Any resemblance to actual events, locales, or persons, living, dead, or otherwise, is coincidental, and extremely unlikely.

Library of Congress Cataloging-in-Publication Data
Allen, William Stuart, 1957-1980
   Swords for hire : two of the most unlikely heroes you'll ever meet / by Will Allen ; [cover painting and book illustrations by David Michael Beck].
     p. cm.
   Summary: In the ancient kingdom of Parmall, sixteen-year-old Sam Hatcher and an eccentric Royal Guard set out on a mission to rescue the rightful king who has been imprisoned in a faraway dungeon by his evil brother.
   ISBN 0-9724882-0-0 (pbk. : alk. paper)
   [1. Fantasy. 2. Adventure and adventurers–Fiction. 3. Humorous stories.] I. Beck, David Michael, 1950-, ill. II. Title.
PZ7.A4388 Sw 2003   2002035163
[Fic]–dc21

CenterPunch Press
P. O. Box 43151
Cincinnati Ohio 45243
www.centerpunchpress.com
Email: info@centerpunchpress.com

Dedicated to my family

Author's note:

*Since this novel is the product of only a first draft
and one rewrite, it may contain a few flaws.
Rather than point them out—you may miss
a few if I don't—I shall cover any and all
objections with the following statement:
I sincerely apologize for writing this book.*

Will Allen

FOREWORD

By Nancy Cartwright, the voice of Bart Simpson

A long, long time ago, before I was playing spiky-headed 10-year-old boys, I had a good friend named Will Allen.

We both grew up in Kettering, Ohio (a little 'burb just south of Dayton). We were both in high school plays and competed on the speech team, better known as "Forensics." Competing in humorous interpretation and dramatic duo, we did so well that we were both awarded scholarships to attend Ohio University in Athens, Ohio.

Once grooved into college life, Will wrote and produced a five-minute daily comedy radio show for the university's radio station. The show was called *Campus,* and featured an eclectic group of characters who lived in "Monty Hall," one of the dorms at the fictional "Marshack University." I played several characters, from Magpie Davenport, a wacky chemistry teacher, to Mrs. Clagg, the drill sergeant-like cafeteria manager.

Every Thursday night, about ten of us would assemble to tape the five shows for the next week. We were crammed into an uncomfortable, unventilated little room, with worn-out recording equipment, and . . . we loved every minute of it. We made over one hundred shows.

In some ways, *Campus* was a glimpse into my future. Flash forward twenty-some years and I'm doing the same thing, assembling with a great group once a week to record some even wackier characters, better known as *The Simpsons.*

Sadly, Will died of cancer in 1980 just as he was finishing college and never had the opportunity to share his talents with a broader audience; however I have no doubt in my mind that Will would have gone on to be a respected writer for film, television and literature. So when Will's brother, Paul, contacted me and said he was going to publish some of Willie's work, I couldn't wait to read this "new" story that had been hidden away for over two decades.

Swords for Hire is vintage Will Allen: It's interesting, surprising, full of suspense and delicious characters, and most of all, funny. I loved it. I couldn't put it down. In fact, my 11-year-old son wouldn't let me put it down! He loved it too! And so will you.

Just one little tip while reading this book to yourself or your kids: Worms do not belong on your head. Keep that in mind and you'll be just fine.

Nancy Cartwright

P.S. Paul is working on publishing more of Will's writing, so stay tuned.

Nancy Cartwright is an Emmy-award winning actress, mother, producer, and voice of Bart, Nelson, Ralph, Todd, Kearney, Database and Maggie on "The Simpsons," and Chuckie on "Rugrats." She is also the best-seller author of "My Life as a 10-Year-Old Boy," an inside look at her career and the making of "The Simpsons."

SWORDS
FOR HIRE

PART 1   # THE KING

ONE

The cell was deep and the cell was dark.

King Olive peered at his cell through bushy eyebrows and wondered just how deep and how dark. Could it be a mile underground? What would be the point of digging so deep? Was it even possible to dig so deep? A half mile also seemed a bit much, so he finally decided that it was a quarter of a mile deep, give or take.

How dark was the cell? Well, Olive realized that he didn't even know the unit of measurement for that, so he settled on "bloody dark enough," and went back to scratching in the dirt by his manacled feet.

He often played little games with himself since there was little else to do, imprisoned as he was. He had estimated the square footage of his cell. He had estimated how many ounces of food he received each day. Once, he even tried to determine the actual nature of the food and its nutritional content, but that made him feel rather ill, and he returned to his previous practice of just closing his eyes and eating.

King Olive was a smallish man, with thick brown hair and a tangled beard. His clothing was the same he had been wearing upon entering the cell three years ago—royal finery, now reduced to rags. Perhaps it was fortunate for Olive's morale that there was no mirror in the cell, for his appearance was generally quite ratty. Even his eyebrows had grown so long that he could hardly see around them. Why, those eyebrows were trimmed every week when he was king . . .

When he was king.

Now and again, King Olive would remember his past glory and his present predicament, and he would rise angrily to his feet, jumping, swearing, pounding at the walls, using up energy that he did not possess. Then, after a long, frustrating fit, he would sink to the floor again in silence.

He stared at his chains and remembered the words his father had spoken on his deathbed.

"You cannot always be right," King Martin had gasped, "but always, my son, *always* be a king."

Upon the death of his father, Prince Olive had become King Olive, the ruler of Parmall. And the new king ruled wisely. His foes often underestimated him because of his small stature, and he was able to hold the throne and rule wisely from it. He could deal with all threats from the outside, never guessing that he would be defeated from within.

King Olive, you see, had a younger brother by the name of Boonder. As children, Olive and Boonder got along well enough, although Olive could never quite understand Boonder's preoccupation with worms.

"I found another worm and I put it on my head," young Boonder would tell his brother.

"Just so you don't eat it," replied Olive uneasily.

But worms were not Boonder's only preoccupation. He was also obsessed with winning. Any game he played, he simply had to win, or he would scream and holler and just carry on something awful. Still, Olive realized that Boonder *was* his brother, and that his tantrums and odd habits had to be lived with.

Boonder was very fond of Olive, too, until the day he realized that his brother, being the eldest, would become the next king. And from that day onward, Boonder's wormy brain began to think very devious thoughts.

*　　*　　*

As King Olive mindlessly tapped at his shackles, he realized for the thousandth time that he should have suspected his brother's treachery. After all, Boonder's betrayal was hardly an original idea. In fact, three good friends of King Olive—King Fordnack, Duke Ruchie, and Archdragoon Phillip—had been similarly removed from power through the cunning of one of their close relatives.

But Olive had no reason at the time to suspect his sibling of anything other than unswerving loyalty. In fact, the king's well-being seemed to be one of Boonder's primary concerns.

"My dear king, if I may have a word with you," said Boonder one morning, bowing deeply.

Olive always winced when his brother called him "my dear king," but he had given up trying to convince Boonder that they were still on a first-name basis.

"Certainly, Boonder. I meet with the ambassador from Proug at ten, but until then I am yours."

"It concerns your health, Sire," said Boonder. Although

now in his thirties, Boonder showed no sign of ever being able to grow a beard or mustache. His smooth, chubby face had emerged from childhood with the baby fat still intact. His black hair was always matted and greasy.

"My health!" laughed Olive. "Boonder, I am strong as an ox and twice as fit. I eat well, work hard, and have even ridden missions with the Royal Guard. Now what would you be telling me?"

Boonder licked his thin lips. "Sire, others have noticed things you may not be aware of. In the past few days, you've been somewhat pale and you've seemed a bit tired."

"Nonsense."

"I don't need to remind you of the vital role you play in Parmall. If you should become seriously ill, even for a week . . . Would you please consent to see a doctor, just as a precaution?"

Olive sighed. If he didn't agree, Boonder would pester him for days. "All right, all right. I'll have the palace physician look me over first chance I get."

"Thank you, m'Lord."

"Boonder, *don't* call me m'Lord!"

Boonder exited, bowing. "Thank you. Thank you."

*   *   *

When the doctor arrived, it looked like Boonder had been right. Old Marnoff, the palace physician, said that King Olive did indeed appear pale and tired. He spoke of "anexious neoplasm" and "infumium panacere." Then he prescribed some round white pills that the King was to take four times daily.

Olive couldn't know, couldn't even guess, that each pill contained a small dose of the rare poison, courem.

TWO

As the days passed, Olive indeed grew more pale and tired. His dear brother came to see him each day and noted the king's gradual decline with satisfaction. The doctor was summoned again. He doubled the dosage.

In a matter of weeks, the king was confined to his bed. He was nauseous much of the time and had a constant headache. During this difficult period, Boonder kindly volunteered to assume many of the king's duties, for which Olive thanked him.

When the king finally went into a coma, Boonder told the doctor to pronounce him dead. There was great mourning in the streets of Parmall, for Olive was truly loved by his people. Candles burned late and minstrels on every corner sang of his mighty and good deeds.

But by morning, the minstrels fell silent and the candles flickered out. It was time for the coronation of the new king to begin.

The people were still filled with sorrow, so there was not as much shouting and celebration as Boonder would have liked. Still, it was a tasteful coronation, and he was now King Boonder. He liked the sound of that. The crown almost slipped off his greasy head, but he caught it and set it back on firmly as he smiled and waved at the crowd.

"My people!" he cried. "Now you are my people, all mine! And I am your king, King Boonder! That's right! And like worms in the rich brown earth, we shall work together to make Parmall great!"

He shook his head wildly, and little flecks of grease flew in all directions. Boonder was so giddy with excitement that it took him several moments to realize that he had nothing else to say. "Well," he said finally, "I guess that's all for now. Just remember, always serve your king!"

It was a somewhat bewildering speech, but after a brief and uncomfortable pause, the crowd applauded anyway.

Boonder presided over a lavish funeral for his brother, but the sealed coffin was, in fact, empty. The real king was sent to the Boneman, an evil friend of Boonder's in a northern land. The Boneman controlled the most impenetrable dungeon in the world. Boonder did not really expect that Olive would recover, but he did not have the courage to end his brother's life himself. So he put the rightful king of Parmall in a crate and had his own personal guards take it over hundreds of rocky miles to the Boneman's dreaded dungeon.

Boonder realized that the fewer people who knew of the plot, the better, so his first official act was to put to death old Marnoff, the palace physician who had conspired with him to eliminate Olive. Boonder knew the kingdom followed him only because he was Olive's brother, so he could not allow anyone else to discover the actual cause of King Olive's demise.

*   *   *

King Olive leaned his head back against the cell's filthy stone wall and wondered if he would feel better if he did not know of his brother's treachery.

No, he decided, it was best to know the truth. And vengeance was at least something to think about.

It was the Boneman who had told him about Boonder. Olive had never seen the Boneman, for his food was always brought by nameless guards, but once, he heard the Boneman's voice. Only once. Shivering, Olive decided that once was enough.

It had happened several months after he arrived. Olive had awakened from his coma upon arriving at the dungeon, but he was very weak. Those first dark months were a blur of pain and nausea. Then, as the poison slowly worked its way out of his system, he began to regain some of his strength.

One evening—Olive fancied it was evening, although it was really impossible to tell—the Boneman came. King Olive heard a heavy thumping coming toward his cell. Finally it stopped just outside.

"Who is it?" Olive whispered. He knew that it was not one of the guards who brought him food and sang bawdy songs. This was someone else.

A harsh laugh and a voice as cold and deep as the grave answered him. *"I am the Boneman,"* the voice rasped. The muscles in King Olive's stomach drew tight like bowstrings.

"I have heard the guards mention you," said Olive, mustering his courage. "You are my captor."

The voice outside the cell shrieked with inhuman laughter. *"Yes! Yes. The Boneman clutches you tightly."*

King Olive tried to draw closer to the door to catch a glimpse of his tormentor, but the chains restrained him. As he pulled futilely against the tempered steel, anger overcame his fear. "Why am I here?" he cried. "I am the king of Parmall, and you have treated me as filth! I demand an explanation!"

There was silence for a moment, and Olive feared that the mysterious man had left. Then the reply came, soft and cold like the rumble of cracking ice on a frozen pond. *"Good. Very well, my trapped animal."* He gave a short, harsh laugh. *"I will tell you."*

King Olive listened silently as the Boneman related Boonder's treachery. Olive knew that it was true, every word. And it made his soul burn.

"That is the story," the Boneman's voice grated. *"I trust it will comfort you on the long nights to come, for they are infinite."*

Olive held his clenched fists tightly against his sides, but he said nothing.

"King," the voice said quietly, *"do you fear me?"*

"Fear you?" Olive raged against his chains. "It is you who should fear me, bag of bones! Fear the day I get out! I will take my revenge on both you and my traitorous brother!"

The Boneman's laughter swelled to a deafening pitch that then faded as he moved down the hallway.

"Fear me, Boneman! Fear me!" Olive cried after him.

But as he sank to his knees on the filthy cell floor, it was Olive who was very much afraid, and without hope.

That had been more than three years ago. Sometimes Olive thought he heard the Boneman's shambling gait outside the cell, but he could never be sure. Still, the mysterious man was a constant visitor to King Olive's dreams. They always ended with Olive turning around to actually *see* the Boneman—and each nightmare brought forth an even more hideous incarnation. In one dream, he was literally a boneman, a screaming skeleton. In others, he became all forms of misshapen creatures, all horribly frightening. All the dreams ended with King Olive awakening with a scream.

Yet because of the constant boredom, he was surprised to find himself sometimes wishing for the Boneman's return. Maybe it would be better to struggle against a monster and die than just . . . rot?

Olive set up a rigid exercise routine to keep his body fit. For a time his goal was to jump as high as the chains around his feet would allow. However, he soon became able to jump even higher. This resulted in very sore ankles and a resolve not to try quite so hard.

He strengthened his arms by pulling at the chains where they were bolted to the stone wall. He knew that neither chains nor wall would budge, but the effort made his arms thick and tough.

The main problem, though, was how to occupy his mind. For a time he drew in the grime at his feet, sketching sunsets and still life. He counted the links of the chains. He tried to count the hairs in his beard, gave up eventually, and settled for counting the hairs in his eyebrows—one thousand, two hundred and sixty-two. Even then, he really only counted one eyebrow and multiplied by two.

He tore a bit of thread from his cloak and learned to tie a variety of knots. Once, after it rained, several spiders found their way into his cell, and he busied himself by learning all about their daily routine, which he decided was much more interesting than his. But most of all, he just stared at the walls.

This particular day—or night, one was never sure— King Olive let his eyes roam across the expanse of the cell and wondered just what he could say about it. The length and width couldn't be noted except in very approximate terms. Besides "rock," he could not be specific as to the materials used in building it. He shrugged wearily. When you got right down to it, there was only one thing to say.

The cell was deep and the cell was dark.

Swords For Hire

THE KING

THE BOY

PART 2

THREE

Meanwhile, hundreds of miles to the south in Parmall, Sam Hatcher was looking over the fence that bordered his father's farm. He stared at the dusty road that in one direction led into town, but in the other direction led . . . where?

Sam smiled wistfully. Why, a person could get on that road and go anywhere! The road disappeared from sight as it wound into the hills, but Sam knew that just beyond those hills exotic adventure awaited.

Sam liked to daydream. In fact, it was one of the things he did best.

Sam Hatcher looked like, well, what he was—a farmer's boy. His sandy hair was chopped each month with the same shears used for the sheep, and his ragged clothes were made for durability rather than style. Still, his body now tottered on the brink of manhood, and his keen eyes and smile seemed to indicate that he was something more than a dull farm boy.

Sam's mother watched him from the door of the farmhouse and sighed. Elsa Hatcher loved Sam more than anything, but he was such an odd boy sometimes. Staring at roads was not a healthy pursuit for a boy of his age.

Or rather, a man of his age, as it was Sam's sixteenth birthday.

"Sam!" she called.

Sam turned.

"Dinner!" As she saw him walking lazily toward her,

she turned and went back inside with a sigh, wondering what would become of him.

By the time Sam had washed up, his mother and father were already seated at the table. Sam smiled and sat down to dinner.

He knew this was no ordinary meal. Oh, the food was nothing surprising—roast pig, potatoes, stringy greens— but the mood was unusual. Sam knew that tonight, his father would have a speech prepared and it might well change Sam's life forever.

Milos Hatcher was a stocky, quiet man. Like his son's, his deep green eyes seemed to glow with perception and wisdom. When Elsa would scoff and shake her head about Sam, Milos would smile quietly to himself.

"The boy's all right," he told his wife one night. "You take my word." Elsa had only shaken her head.

The meal passed in complete silence. Outside, twilight imperceptibly began to turn to night. One by one, insects began their chorus, and then the meal was over. Had it taken forever, or had they eaten it all in a few mad gulps?

"Today you have become a man, Sam," said his father. "Congratulations."

"Thank you, Father."

Milos scratched his chin thoughtfully. "Why don't we take a little walk?"

Sam nodded.

"Elsa, we'll be back shortly," Milos said.

"Fine," Elsa replied quietly. But as she watched them step out into the darkness, she knew that Sam would never be back, at least not as a child that she could cry and fuss over and order about. She was gaining a man but losing her baby, and it brought tears to her eyes. The soft sound of her sorrow did not reach those outside.

"Sam," Milos said as they walked beneath the stars, "what do you see yourself doing over the next . . . oh, five or ten years?"

Sam looked at his father. "I really don't know. I suppose I should . . . but I don't."

His father nodded as they continued to walk. "Well, that's an honest answer." He paused to spit out a piece of gristle caught between his teeth. "You've been helping out on the farm since you were a baby. How do you like farming?"

Sam was surprised at the question. "I like it a lot . . ."

"No you don't," his father cut him off. "No, for you farming is something to do while you wait for something better to come along. Some men love it, of course. You can see that connection between them and the soil. When a real farmer scoops up a handful of dirt, you can see something special in his eyes. He knows the land, he loves it, it's what makes him whole."

"And that's . . . not me."

"You know that's not you. When you're planting or plowing, your eyes are on the sky, not the ground." Milos filled his pipe, tapped the tobacco down, and lit it before continuing.

"You know," he said, "before I was a farmer, before you were born, I was a member of the Royal Guard."

Sam looked at his father and was proud. Proud that years before, Milos Hatcher had been one of the ten highest-skilled fighting men in all of Parmall.

For that is indeed what the Royal Guard was: A team of the mightiest, strongest, and bravest men in the kingdom, handpicked to protect the king and overcome any danger to the realm. Tales of the brave adventures of these green-clad heroes were many, from saving a member of the royal family from an assassination plot, to going on a quest to a far-off land.

Milos Hatcher had been a guardsman for three years. His service to King Martin, King Olive's father, had been cut short when he received several sword-thrusts intended for the king. It was feared that he would die from them, but somehow he had regained his health, due in part to Elsa, the caring nurse who had later become his wife.

But he would never fight again.

The wounds had ruined the delicate balance required for true fighting skill. Milos was still strong, but his body had been robbed of its former coordination. As a tribute to his bravery, King Martin had given him a large farm and several servants. As the years went by, Milos had set the servants free but kept the farm.

Though he was now only a farmer, there was a special light in Milos Hatcher's eyes when he looked at his son and said, "Have you ever thought about joining the Royal Guard?"

Sam was incredulous. The calm father-son chat had just taken an absurd turn.

"Me? You're kidding."

"Am I?" said his father.

FOUR

Reluctantly, Sam found himself the next morning at the headquarters of the Royal Guard, which was located within the very walls of the palace. King Boonder himself must be somewhere inside, Sam realized.

He had an appointment to see the captain of the guard, but for some unknown reason he was forced to wait for hours in a vast hall. Decorated with tapestries and lined with intricately carved wood bookshelves, mostly the hall was just big and made Sam feel small.

Finally the large doors at one end swung open. A distant voice said, "Captain Clerret will see you now."

The captain was thinner than Sam had imagined. Still, his handshake was stronger than his slim frame implied. Although his beard was gray, there was fire in his eyes. He wore the traditional green of the Royal Guard.

"Sit down, sit!" he said gruffly. Sam obeyed, but the captain seemed to lose all interest in him. The old man perused the notes on his desk for such a long time that Sam was about to clear his throat when the captain looked up suddenly.

"So!" he said, "you are the son of Milos Hatcher."

"Yes, sir," Sam began, "I . . ."

"Quick!" snapped Clerret, "How do you disembowel a horse?"

Sam's mouth dropped. "Sir?"

"Next question! Where can you press on the human body and instantly render the person senseless?"

"Uh . . . the eyeball?"

"Wrong! Last question: How can a cup of water be made into a deadly weapon?"

"Captain Clerret, I . . ."

"Wrong again! All wrong!" the man said with malicious glee. Then he leaned forward on his desk. "Don't repeat those questions to anyone. They're my favorites."

"Yes, sir," said Sam uneasily.

Captain Clerret drew a cigar from his right-hand drawer, lit it, and leaned back with a smile. "Had enough of the scare tactics?"

Sam nodded. "I think so."

"Fine," Clerret said. "I just do that to keep you on your toes. Expect the unexpected! Now, boy, what can I do for you?"

Sam tried to regain his composure. "Well, sir, my father suggested that I seek employ in the ranks of the Royal Guard."

Clerret leaned back and blew smoke through his thick beard. "Ah yes, old Milos Hatcher. Young Milos then, we were all young then." He stared at the ceiling and shook his head slowly, remembering the days of King Martin. His gaze returned to Sam. "Now, King Martin, *there* was a king! His son, Olive, too. A fine ruler, proud to serve him. Now with that blasted Boonder, there's no respect to this job."

Sam leaned forward. "I thought Boonder was a good king."

"Who told you so?"

"Well, he did, in his speeches."

"Ah, the man's an idiot. Puts worms on his head. Worms! It's no fun being part of the Royal Guard when the King puts worms on his head!"

Sam shook his head. "I had no idea."

Captain Clerret sighed. "Well, keep it that way. You didn't hear a word about Boonder from me, understand?"

"You can trust me."

"Good," said the old man, leaning back in his chair. "Now, about joining the Royal Guard . . . do you have any military experience?"

"No, sir," Sam said softly. I should have never come, he thought, this is ridiculous!

Clerret scratched his beard. "Hmmm. That makes for a bit of a problem. Ever kill anyone?"

"I've slaughtered hogs," Sam said hopefully.

"Hogs, hogs, that's good, that's a start." Then the captain's face fell. "Look here, young man, I can't lead you on. The Royal Guard is the military's top—men who have trained and fought all their lives. Not farm boys with military fathers."

Sam nodded and tried to smile. "I know, sir. Thank you for seeing me."

Clerret stood to see the boy out. "Quite all right. No bother at all. Come back again and bring some cigars."

"Thanks again," Sam said.

The old man started to nod, then looked at Sam. "Wait," he said. "For an old friend's son, perhaps we can work something else out."

Sam winced. He had guessed this was coming. "You mean enlist as a common footsoldier? I don't think . . ."

Captain Clerret shook his head. "No, no, no."

Sam's eyes widened. "You mean you'll let me in the Guard?"

Captain Clerret shook his head again, more violently this time. "Heavens, no. You just wouldn't fit in, but you see, you're not the only one."

"Sir?"

Captain Clerret leaned forward. "Four years ago King Olive's life was saved by a young man. The plot was heinous, and it was a combination of sheer luck and spunk that enabled the man to save Olive's life. To repay him, Olive made the man a member of the Royal Guard. However, we soon found that he didn't really fit in with our setup here. He wouldn't march, he had many . . . odd personal habits and the like. A very nice young man, you understand, just . . . different. Have a cigar?"

"No, thank you."

"Mmmm. Anyway, I could hardly remove him from the Guard after the King put him there, so we established him as a special unit of one. He mostly does whatever he wants. If he can find a quest, he's welcome to it. If he merely wants to patrol the streets, that's fine too. He doesn't bother us and we don't bother him."

Sam straightened. "What does this have to do with me?"

Clerret smiled. "If he'll take you on as an apprentice, perhaps you could get some experience and then come back to us later."

Sam swallowed. "Are you sure he'll take me on?"

The old man shook his head. "That I can't say. He's the most unpredictable man I've ever met. But maybe he'll give you a try."

It didn't sound all that appealing, but Sam saw no other alternatives at the moment. "Well . . ."

"Very good. Here, I'll sketch you out some directions so you can find him."

Sam nodded. "Oh, by the way, sir . . . what is this man's name?"

Captain Clerret looked up from his papers. "Rigby Skeet."

"Rigby . . . ?"

"Rigby Skeet," Clerret repeated

" . . . Interesting name," said Sam.

"Interesting man," replied Clerret.

FIVE

King Boonder sat on his throne. Before him stood the royal jeweler. "Does his majesty like the gold ring I have crafted?" asked the hunched-over man from behind tiny spectacles.

Boonder aimlessly fingered the priceless ring. "Oh, it's all right, I suppose."

The jeweler's eyes seemed to become larger than his glasses. "But Sire! I spent two months crafting that ring! It's the crowning work of my life."

Boonder tossed the ring up in the air and tried to catch it, but missed. It struck the floor with a tiny thud. The king frowned.

The old man was in tears. "What could possibly please you? Each time I bring you a work more precious and magnificent than the last, and each time you are more disappointed! Sire, what is it you want? I am the finest jeweler in the realm. Tell me what you want."

"Let me think a minute," Boonder said.

"Take your time," the little man said, exasperated.

Boonder leaned forward in deep thought. After a moment, he brightened. "Can you make me a worm?"

"A what!"

"A worm!" Boonder said excitedly. "A glorious golden worm with diamonds for eyes!"

"You mean like a worm you dig out of the garden?"

"Yes! Except the worm you make will be priceless—and the only one of its kind! I shall own the most priceless worm in all the world!"

The jeweler stared at the ground. "Err—what size would you like it?"

Boonder stroked his chin. "Better make it five times bigger so all the details really show."

The jeweler turned to leave. "Aye, m'Lord. I'll get right to work."

"There's one more thing."

"Yes?"

King Boonder removed the crown from his greasy head. "Could you get me some clips for this or something? It keeps sliding off my head."

The old man suppressed his disgust. "Certainly, Sire." He turned and left the throne room, resolved, at least for the moment, to do himself in rather than succumb to such degradation. Golden worms and grease clips indeed!

"King Boonder, might I have a word?" It was Lord Aleron, Boonder's top advisor.

Boonder had been picking his nose and quickly tried to make it appear as if he was only scratching. "Of course, come in, Aleron."

Lord Aleron was tall and dark-haired, with a smooth clean-shaven face. He was an important statesman and looked the part. He smiled as he spoke. "I have just visited the civil offices, and the annual collection of taxes seems to be going right on schedule."

Boonder nodded. "Excellent."

"Also," Aleron continued, "our investigation of the

slaying of one of our soldiers near the Surrenk border revealed that the incident was not a provocation of war by the Surrenkians, but rather a bandit raid. Still, I've doubled our patrols in that region to make sure there is no reoccurrence."

Boonder wasn't sure he could remember the initial incident, but he nodded anyway. "Fine."

"And finally," said Aleron, "I consulted with three representatives of the Maresh Kingdom and worked out a mutually beneficial system of trade. I have the details right here if you'd care to . . ."

"No, no," Boonder said, waving his hands. "It's all too much for me. Aleron, I really don't know what I'd do without you."

Lord Aleron smiled. "I was proud to serve your brother and I am now proud to serve you."

Boonder tried not to let his expression change. "Yes, dear Olive . . . "

Aleron shook his head wistfully. "If only he could see the fine manner in which you rule. He would be proud."

"Yes, I do miss my dear brother." Boonder bowed his head.

The crown hit the floor with a tremendous clatter.

"I hate that slippery thing!" shouted Boonder.

Aleron bent to pick it up. "Here you are, Sire. It doesn't appear to be damaged."

Boonder was flustered and had no desire for continued conversation. "Yes, yes—well, thank you for that report, Aleron. I shall speak with you again very soon."

"Aye, Sire," said Aleron, bowing. "I have several other important matters to attend to for you this afternoon. As always, I shall seek your counsel if there are difficulties."

"Very good, very good," said Boonder, waving Aleron away.

The door closed and King Boonder was alone once more. He sat in a cushioned throne in the midst of royal splendor. For his slightest whim, he had but to ask. For a moment he thought of his brother Olive, rotting away in a dark bare cell, eating bowls of slop unfit for human consumption.

For a moment it bothered him.

But only for a moment.

Soon his thoughts drifted to the sumptuous dinner that awaited him. He idly thought that one of these days he should make another speech to the populace. It also occurred to him that it had been weeks since he had washed his hair.

"Tonight," Boonder said aloud with an air of resolve, "I shall wash my hair."

But he didn't.

Swords For Hire

THE KING

THE BOY

PART 3 **THE ODDBALL**

Six

Following the directions Captain Clerret had given him, Sam Hatcher proceeded to Rigby Skeet's house.

This is crazy, Sam thought as he walked. When did I decide to be a warrior? All I know is a little farming. I never thought I'd grow up to be . . .

Conflicting thoughts ran through his head, but he decided to continue, if only to please his father. "Rigby Skeet, here I come," he said aloud.

Following the map, Sam turned onto an overgrown path that led away from the village. Soon a small dwelling appeared. As Sam drew closer, he saw that the house had fallen into disrepair. The roof sported several small holes and a couple of gaping ones. The door was cracked and splintered. Indeed it was little more than a shack.

As he drew still closer, he noticed a small placard by the door that read *Rigby Skeet, Sword For Hire.*

Sam sighed and knocked on the door.

He heard a clunking noise inside, then the door opened to reveal a man who looked to be in his mid-thirties, with coarse dark hair and a beard to match.

"Yes?" the man said.

Sam cleared his throat. "I'm looking for Rigby Skeet."

The man picked a bug off his tunic, looked for a moment as if he were going to eat it, then tossed it to the ground. "Seek no further, farm boy." He stepped back and bowed graciously. "You have found him."

Sam smiled. "I'm pleased to meet you . . ."

Rigby Skeet suddenly hurled himself backward and drew his sword as a crazed look came into his eyes. "Then, varlet," he snarled, "Tell me what business it is you have with the mighty Rigby Skeet, the greatest swordsman in all of Parmall!" With a yell, he swung the heavy sword and chopped the door in half from top to bottom.

Sam stood aghast.

Rigby Skeet paused, looking first at his sword and then at the door. "Rats," he said. He looked back at Sam. "Anyway, where were we? Ah, yes. I was about to either run you through or save you from perils more horrible than any man has ever known. Depending on your reasons for being here, of course. Actually, I hope you have some sort of great quest for me. Quests are hard to come by these days, and while running someone through is sometimes interesting, it's over like *that*." He punctuated the last word by slashing the remainder of the door with his sword. "Double rats."

Sam swallowed. "Uhh . . . Captain Clerret sent me, Sir Skeet."

"Please. Rigby."

"Very well, Rigby." Sam went on to relate what had transpired and why he was here.

Rigby stroked his beard. "I see. Well, come in and sit and we shall discuss it."

The interior of the shack was much like the exterior. Dust was settled over much of the place. Rigby and Sam sat down in wooden chairs near the fireplace.

"Care for some wine?" Rigby asked.

"No, thank you."

"That's a lucky thing," said Rigby. "I'm all out. It's really not all that glamorous a life, being a sword for hire. Frankly, since they kindly removed me from the Royal Guard, I've been rather on the skids, workwise. I mean, a person can put a 'Sword for Hire' sign on his door from now until the cows come home, but that doesn't mean he'll get any business. Are you cold? Shall I start up the fire?"

Sam was getting more confused by the minute. "No, thank you."

Rigby leaned forward. "Would you like to know the exact amount of work I've done in the last three years? Nothing. Zip. Zero. Nada. Oh, sure, I helped catch those rogues that escaped from the prison, and I skewered a rabid dog, and I helped some old lady and her cats out of a burning house, but that's not true adventure! You know, I want to lop the ears off giants and fight off an army when the odds are two thousand to one against me. Stuff like that. Real fun!"

Sam stood abruptly. "Sir . . . uh, Rigby . . . I thank you for your consideration, but I think I've made a mistake in coming to see you."

"Sit down!" Rigby said coldly. "Nobody stands up abruptly in front of me."

Sam sat. "I'm sorry. It's just that . . . well, my father was in the Royal Guard. It was he who wanted me to do this, not me. I'm no warrior."

Rigby spat. "What you're trying to tell me, kid, is that

you're not man enough to sword around with me."

Sam lowered his head. "Yes."

Rigby stood up and kicked his chair against the fireplace. "No, no, no! You stupid farmer, the least you can do is argue!"

Sam looked up angrily. "You said yourself you never do anything exciting or heroic! Why should I stay around here?"

Rigby leaned close to Sam. "Because you got it, kid. I could tell the second you walked in the door."

"Got what?"

Rigby slammed a fist against the wall. "It, boy, it! That magical, mystical something! Are you sure you're not hungry?"

Sam stood up. "I'm not hungry! What are you talking about?"

"Got me," said Rigby. "But let me tell you, boy, it came from the heart. You got potential, I can't say how I know, but I do."

Sam shook his head. "If I have such great potential, shouldn't my first move be to get out of this crummy shack?"

"SHACK?" thundered Rigby. "I'll have you know I built this place with my own two hands! Actually, that's a lie, it's been here since before I was born. But I've been taking care of it lately."

Sam laughed. "Captain Clerret was right. You *are* crazy."

Rigby looked for an instant as though he might be angry, but then he smiled. He walked to the window and looked out. "Join me, boy," he said softly. "I guarantee you an interesting time."

"I don't doubt that," said Sam. He was silent for a moment, but only a moment. His only alternative was to return to the farm.

"All right. I'm your pupil in the manly arts of destruction and mayhem."

Rigby smiled. "That's fine. All right, then, pupil. First we must get a few rules straight. Prepare for your first lesson."

Sam sat back down and shrugged. "I'm ready."

"Good. Rule number one: Rigby Skeet is now your personal deity. In the morning and before meals you shall pray aloud—'Hail Rigby Skeet, lord of all the universe.' "

"What!"

Rigby sighed. "Oh, all right. Forget rule number one. Rule number two: Each morning, to prove your bravery and fearlessness, you shall kill either a cat, a dog, or a small child."

"That's horrible!"

Rigby looked annoyed. "Well, of course it is. It wouldn't be an act of bravery if it weren't, now would it?"

"I refuse to take part in . . . in . . . "

Rigby nodded. "Such a barbaric act. Very well, very well, we'll strike rule two also. Rule number three: To prove your toughness, you must, at every opportunity, take part in cannibalism."

Sam stood up. "Utterly preposterous!"

Rigby looked hurt. "Not even just a little cannibalism?

On weekends?"

"Certainly not!"

"Oh, all right." Rigby rubbed his head. "Well, that's all the rules I have."

"Thank God," said Sam.

They sat in silence until Sam finally said, "Well, what are we going to do with ourselves?"

Rigby took a stick from his pocket and began to chew on it. "Well, I suppose I'll start out by teaching you the fundamentals. How to wield a sword, how to string and shoot a bow, hand-to-hand combat. Uh, do you know how to read?"

"Of course," said Sam.

"Good," said Rigby. "You can teach me. I'll also teach you battle strategy, survival techniques, and so on."

"You know," said Sam, "I didn't think I'd like this at all, but at least it sounds interesting. Do you think we'll get to work on any actual quests?"

Rigby frowned. "Well, as I say, boy, it's been pretty slow lately, but you never know when duty may call."

At that instant, a man with three arrows in his body staggered in through the open doorway, gasped, and fell to the floor.

Rigby looked at Sam. "See what I mean?"

SEVEN

Sam was as pale as bleached muslin. "Is he dead?"

Rigby moved toward the still figure on the floor. "Three arrows in him—if he's not dead now, it's just a matter of time."

Sam turned away and put a hand to his stomach, feeling nauseous. Was this the adventure he had sought? He suddenly wished he was back on the farm, slopping the hogs, shearing the sheep . . .

Rigby stood, shaking his head. "Poor soul's dead, all right. A pity—he probably had something important to say." He turned to Sam. "Be a good little student, Sam, and go to the window to see if there are any more murderous bowmen out there with their sights on us."

"Us?" yelped Sam.

Rigby nodded. "It's possible. Now hurry, give a look while I see if this gentleman has anything of interest on his person."

Sam accepted his new role of hero as best he could. He crept up to the window and then quickly peeked outside, half certain that he would receive an arrow in his nose. But he did not, nor did he see anyone. He cautiously moved to check out the other window, then the door. The wind moved softly through the trees, somewhere a dog was barking, but there was no sign of enemy attack.

Sam turned to Rigby. "Looks all clear to me."

"Fine," said Rigby. "I think I may have found . . ."

"Pardon me," said a harsh voice.

Three warriors stood at the door, each armed with a large broadsword and wearing a distinctive black tunic.

Rigby turned to Sam. "Looks all clear to me?"

"I . . . I don't know where they could have come from," Sam sputtered.

Rigby turned back to the menacing-looking visitors. "Sorry, boys, the Warriors' Convention is three doors down. Not counting this door," he said, "which is no longer much of a door at all, if you get my driftwood."

The leader of the trio stepped forward. "You two have captured and killed the murderer, Krendan, who slaughtered six people, including two small children, in the Honar province. At last our long search is ended."

Sam, who had started breathing again, stepped forward. "You mean this . . . dead man on the floor here is a wanted criminal?"

"Exactly," said the leader. "Now he has met retribution for his crimes." He pulled a small piece of paper from a pocket. "I must have your names."

Rigby waved a hand in the air. "Hold it, hold it there just a second. First of all, we didn't capture or kill this gentleman. He stumbled into my humble abode mere minutes ago with three arrows already in place. Second, who are you?"

The leader rubbed a hand over his cheek, which looked like aged leather. "I am Captain Sarbak, of the King's Elite."

Rigby cocked his head sideways, as dogs sometimes do. "You mean the Royal Guard?"

"No. The King's Elite was recently formed by King Boonder. It is a higher post than the Royal Guard."

Rigby shrugged. "First I've heard of it. But I'm sure you've heard of me, for I'm none other than Rigby Skeet, free agent of the Royal Guard, sword for hire, the man for whom no job is too small! I fight for truth, for freedom, for little bunnies with pink eyes!"

Sarbak frowned and made a notation. Then he looked at Sam. "And you?"

"Sam Hatcher, sir. Mr. Skeet is going to teach me everything he knows."

Sarbak laughed quietly and made another notation. "Very well," he said. "You shall each receive a monetary reward for your part in Krendan's capture."

Sam sat down and mopped his brow. They wouldn't be killed after all! In fact, they would be rewarded just because a man had happened to die here. Still, Sam couldn't bring himself to feel good. He was relieved but still confused.

"Can I get you guys a cup of tea or something?" asked Rigby.

"No," Sarbak said curtly. "We must be on our way. Thank you for your help and please mention this to no one. Krendan's apprehension has . . . political repercussions." He turned to the two men behind him. "Get the body."

As the soldiers moved to lift the dead man, Sam said, "But I still don't understand. Who killed this man if you didn't and we didn't?"

For the first time, Captain Sarbak seemed at a loss. "Well, it could have been some local boys learning to use a bow and arrow and, well . . . getting a bit out of hand."

Sam shook his head. "You mean like human target practice? Sounds a bit unlikely."

Rigby stood with a smile. "On the contrary, Sam-boy, it happens all the time! The most deadly creatures on God's green earth are adolescent schoolboys learning to use dangerous weapons! When you teach a boy to use an axe, better lock up the dogs and cats or you'll find them in pieces on the back porch!"

"Yes. We must leave. You will receive your reward by special messenger. Thank you once again," Sarbak said.

With that, the two silent soldiers dragged the body out of the house, followed by their leader, who bowed as he exited.

Rigby shook his head. "Got my floor all bloody. Have to see if I can get a rug to cover that. It won't all wash out, that's for sure."

Sam rubbed his eyes in tired bewilderment. "I feel like I've been dreaming. What happened here?"

Rigby spat into the fireplace. "Can I get you a cup of that tea now?"

"Yes. Yes, I think so."

Rigby moved to a cupboard, opened it, and began rummaging through the various items contained therein. "Blast," he said. "I'm fresh out of tea. Well, I'm glad those goons didn't want any. Probably would have lopped off my head when they found out all I had to offer them was hot water." He turned to Sam. "You want some hot water?"

Sam shrugged. "Well . . . "

"I can put some leaves in it, if you like."

"Tea leaves?"

"No . . . oak, maple, like that."

Sam paused, then said, "Just the water, I guess."

EIGHT

Neither man spoke as Rigby started the fire and set the pot on. It was dusk outside, and the crackling fire added needed warmth and light to the room. Finally the water was ready. Rigby handed Sam a cup and poured one for himself.

"They were lying, you know," he said.

"Who was?"

"Captain Guacamole and his bloody Elite Corps."

"What were they lying about? OW! This stuff is hot!"

Rigby nodded. "Let it set a minute. Here, I think I got a little bread and cheese, too." He went to the cupboard and returned with some chunks of bread and cheese. He tore them into small pieces and handed half to Sam. "There. A regular meal."

Sam smiled. "Thanks. Just like Mom used to make."

Rigby bit off a hunk of bread. "I'll bet. Anyway, those soldier fellows were lying about everything."

"How do you know?"

Rigby stirred the fire with a stick. As it blazed anew, the light danced across his face. "I'll take it from the top, more or less, though I'm not known for my logical progression of thought. First, our dead man, Krendan, is supposed to be from the Honar province. Well, his clothes aren't right for the Honar province. Also, most Honar males have their ears pierced for some ungodly reason. Our man didn't."

Sam blew across the hot liquid, then took a sip. "Well,

neither of those is definite proof."

Rigby smiled. "Quite so, but the arrows piercing the poor man's body didn't belong to any pack of deranged boys."

"But you said . . . "

"I said I believed them!" Rigby laughed. "Of course! What was I supposed to say to three heavily-armed goons? No, best they think us harmless."

Sam nodded. "The captain did seem a bit ill at ease about the whole thing."

"And with good reason," Rigby agreed. "Those arrows are . . . well, they're the finest made. Crofite tip, chillum shaft, precision balanced. Expensive, too. Soldiers who can afford them make it a point to dig them out of the enemy after they do their work."

Sam pulled his chair closer to the fire as a chill wind brushed his back. "Whose arrows were they, then?"

Rigby spat in the fire and listened to the crackle. "My money's on those three high and mighty King's Elite."

"But they didn't have bows or quivers."

Rigby Skeet stood up angrily and kicked his chair over. "Come on, plow-boy! You're off the farm now, use your head! Couldn't they have stashed them before they came in?"

"It's possible," Sam answered coldly.

Rigby tugged at his beard. "Yes, indeed, it's possible, my love."

Sam did not enjoy being treated like a child, especially since he was now legally a man. "Just a minute," he said.

"There's no need to yell at me. Even with all your glorious facts and deductions, we have no proof whatsoever that the dead man was not Krendan, or that the Elite killed him! Someone else, maybe a renegade soldier, could have had those arrows." Sam paused and lowered his voice. "Or perhaps you're just a little too anxious to find an adventure again. Been sitting on your sword-for-hire duff just a little too long."

Rigby turned away from Sam and stared into the fire. The silence grew and neither had the courage to break it. The sun was setting outside, and the room grew slowly colder.

Sam Hatcher sat very still, wondering again what he was doing here, wondering why he couldn't keep his big fat mouth shut. He thought of the farm, of his parents, and of the warm meal his mother must be preparing. He remembered how he used to stare at the road and dream of leaving one day. Now that he had left, where had that magical road brought him?

Rigby Skeet stood facing the fire. It was obvious that he was a very muscular man, a fact which was often hidden by his odd mannerisms and loose clothing. Sam could not tell what was going on in his mind.

Rigby turned. "Sam," he said quietly, "You know, you could be right." And then, a broad smile burst out on his face. "You could be—but you're not."

Sam couldn't help smiling; it was infectious. "What do you mean?"

Rigby reached into his pocket. "Before the goons

arrived, I found a little piece of evidence on the body of the dead man that explains why King Boonder's Elite wanted him dead." He held up a folded piece of paper.

Sam waved a hand in the air. "Well, don't keep me in suspense! What is it?"

"It's a note," Rigby said, "from King Olive."

"What?"

"That's right," Rigby said, leaning forward and grinning. "He's alive."

Swords For Hire

NINE

King Olive was indeed alive, alone and rotting in a deep, dark cell.

If you can call that living.

But now he felt an odd sense of hope, for he had indeed sent a note to the outside world. The scheme through which he got the tiny sliver of paper, wrote on it, and smuggled it out was so complicated that the details would take dozens of pages to describe. Suffice it to say that it took Olive four months to conceive the plan and another five to execute it. The plan involved his own blood and fingernails, a trainable rodent, and a drain-pipe. All things considered, it was the second most amazing thing to ever happen.

The first was that the Boneman found out about it.

"Swine!" The Boneman's cold voice shrieked from the corridor, *"You have sent out a message!"*

King Olive laughed. He had hope now, and his health was improving because of it. "What are you going to do, Boneman? Lock me in a cell?"

"Never laugh at me," warned the voice from the grave. *"You will be given no food tomorrow."*

Olive swallowed. The food was far from good, but he needed it to sustain himself. He would suffer for the flip comment.

He heard a clicking, shambling sound from the hall and wondered again what the Boneman looked like. Olive still feared him very much.

Suddenly the Boneman let out a hideous, shrieking laugh. *"Your efforts were in vain! We will stop any message."* A pause, broken only by the Boneman's heavy breathing. *"You will be here forever, my king."*

As the Boneman's heavy footsteps receded, Olive pulled futilely against his manacles. He knew that he would not have another chance to send a message. Drain pipes would be closed off, rats would be exterminated. His only hope was that, somehow, the message had gotten out.

Tears ran down King Olive's cheeks, and all his manly courage could not stop them.

*   *   *

Boonder had been a nervous wreck since he received a message from the Boneman warning of Olive's scheme. How on earth had Olive gotten a message out? This could be the end of everything!

When he was alone, Boonder put big worms on his head, but even that did not relax him. He knew that if a message from Olive had gotten out, it would mean the end of his reign and possibly his life as well.

It was then that he had quickly formed the King's Elite, a group of ten cutthroats and assassins. Boonder knew he could not use the Royal Guard for this mission, since they might still be faithful to Olive. In addition, the Elite would not be bothered by legalities.

It was twilight in Parmall, and Boonder sat fidgeting on his throne, biting his fingernails and waiting for some word from the Elite.

Suddenly, Captain Sarbak kicked open the door and threw a corpse onto the palace floor, where it went *splat*. Boonder's stomach heaved, and he let out a low moan.

Sarbak smiled. You could tell he smiled only when someone else was uncomfortable or in pain. "This man was bringing a message from your late brother," Sarbak said. "It seems he had a little accident."

Boonder fingered his greasy hair nervously. "So I see." The idea of murder made him queasy—after all, he hadn't killed Olive. But this, he realized, was necessary. "Did he have a chance to speak to anyone?"

Captain Sarbak fingered the handle of his sheathed sword. "Doubtful. But it is possible. There were these two misfits in a shack . . ."

"Have them taken care of at once!" Boonder realized that he was getting flustered. He would feel much better after all this was over and done with.

Captain Sarbak kicked the corpse at his feet. "You underestimate me, King. It's being taken care of as we speak."

Boonder eased back in his throne. "Good."

Suddenly the door swung open, and Lord Aleron walked in. His eyes fell to the bloody corpse and he instantly turned away in shock.

Boonder was taken aback. "Aleron . . ."

"Sire, what is the meaning of this? What happened to this man?"

Boonder wanted time to think of a reasonable answer

but realized that any hesitation would betray his own guilt. "This man had some horrible sort of accident," he explained. "Captain Sarbak of my Elite Guard is taking care of it."

Captain Sarbak stood quietly, hand on sword.

Lord Aleron nodded uncertainly. "You're sure I can't help you investigate this matter?"

Boonder shook his head vigorously. "No, my Elite can handle the problem."

Lord Aleron glanced at Captain Sarbak and then turned back to the King. "As you wish, Sire. I will return with these matters of state at a later time, when you are free. By your leave." Aleron bowed and exited.

Boonder sighed. Lord Aleron was a good man, and even somewhat of a friend. He kept the kingdom running smoothly, handling the many things that Boonder either knew nothing about or had no interest in. At Boonder's request, he had even drafted the members of the King's Elite, including Captain Sarbak. But if he suspected anything . . .

"Shall I kill him for you?" Sarbak asked.

"No," Boonder said. "Not yet."

THE KING

THE BOY

THE ODDBALL

PART 4　　　　　　THE NOTE

TEN

"But that's impossible," Sam said. "King Olive died over three years ago, or hadn't you heard?"

Rigby put a fatherly hand on Sam's shoulder. "Well, you know, my small friend, one gets to do quite a few things as a member of the Royal Guard, and one of them is delivering messages from the king. Now you can roll me into a ball and kick me down a well, but this is Olive's handwriting, so help me God."

Sam was confused again, and the muscles in his face that registered confusion were starting to get pretty sore. "Well, what does it say, anyway?"

"You forget, boy, I can't read," said Rigby. "But I *know* this is Olive's handwriting—I recognize his signature— and it appears to be written in blood." Handing the note to Sam, he added, "You'll have to tell *me* what it says."

Sam took the note and moved closer to the fire. He held the small, weather-beaten note gingerly toward the light and read aloud.

"To any just man: I am the rightful King of Parmall. Although reported dead, I am alive. My death was staged by my brother, Boonder. I am in a cell somewhere to the north of Parmall. My captor is called the Boneman. Notify those who are loyal to me. I wish not so much for my own freedom, but for my treacherous brother to face justice. King Olive of Parmall."

Sam looked at Rigby. "You really think he's alive?"

"Yes."

"But how can you explain . . . how could everyone be taken in? I mean, he was buried! It's hard to believe that . . ."

"Shut up!"

"Just because you don't agree with what I say . . ."

"Sam, *quiet.*"

Rigby seemed to be listening very carefully, but Sam could only hear the steady chirp of crickets.

Rigby spoke very quickly and quietly. "Okay. They'll either come in the door and chop us into little pieces, or they'll burn the house down. If we're lucky, they'll go for the house. Easier for them to explain tomorrow."

Sam felt himself grow cold. "Who? What do you mean?"

Rigby paused again, listening, then he pulled Sam toward one of the back corners of the shack. "Unless I miss my guess, some of our Elite friends are back. They can't take the chance that we got some information from the dead man." He spat. "Probably been watching this place since they left."

Sam felt as he imagined a pig headed for slaughter must feel. "They're going to kill us?"

"I think they're going to give it their best shot," Rigby replied. "Here, help me move this," he added, pushing a heavy wooden chest out of the corner.

Sam moved to help. "Why don't we make a run for it?"

"Haven't you had enough of crofite-tipped arrows for one day?"

Sam moved a cold hand across his face. "Then we're trapped."

Rigby gripped Sam's shoulder. "Hey, chin up, kid,

you're with the original sword for hire. Back there in the corner, where the chest was, if you pull up some boards, you'll see a tunnel."

"A tunnel?"

Suddenly the silence was broken by a sharp utterance coming from somewhere outside the shack.

Rigby scowled. "Okay, we'll have to make this quick. Our fire has died down, that's good, they won't be able to see us. Any minute now they'll torch the house. The instant the first torch hits, we pry up those boards and go for the tunnel. We can't do it before then, it would be too noisy. Hopefully the fire will make enough noise to cover us."

"Where does the tunnel go?"

"Back into the woods, about twenty yards. Now . . . "

WHOOSH.

Outside, the first torch had made its spiral through the air and settled on the roof of the shack.

"Help me with this, *quietly*," said Rigby, already starting to pry up a board.

WHOOSH.

A second torch landed by the side of the house, the flames licking upward with surprising speed.

WHOOSH.

The third torch went in the open doorway, illuminating all within.

"They can see in now," hissed Rigby. "Move."

Two more torches were thrown, and the night became alive with light. The spreading fire crackled with delight as the old structure groaned.

Six black garbed King's Elite surrounded the house, each with a drawn bow. Against the burning house, anyone trying to escape would be a clearly defined target, but no one emerged. The flames were everywhere now, engulfing the house.

One of the Elite relaxed his bow. "That's enough, ain't it? Nobody's gonna walk away from *that*."

"Sarbak told us to wait until we're certain," the group's leader said.

"But people from the village are going to see this and be here any minute!" complained the soldier.

"I said we wait!"

A scant seven minutes later, the flimsy wooden structure collapsed in an abrupt explosion of sparks. Only blackened, flame-licked embers remained.

The leader returned his arrow to his quiver and smiled. "All right," he said, "*now* we can go."

ELEVEN

They were still on the move when dawn finally came. They had kept up a good pace through the night, moving off the main roads only when someone approached. But now, as the sun rose, they took to the woods. It was slow going.

"I'm hungry," said Sam.

Rigby didn't respond. They had been silent through most of the night.

Sam tried in vain to brush some of the dirt off his clothes. "I'm tired, too," he added.

Rigby looked at him with a grin and spat. "Poor baby."

They continued on, numbly forcing their way through the thick underbrush. Sam caught his foot on a root and stumbled. Rigby helped steady him.

"We have a better chance of not being seen back here, but we're leaving a trail a mile long," Rigby said.

"Then why don't we stop?"

Rigby fingered his beard. "Maybe we should, but I think it's probably best to put a lot of distance between us and the Elite bunch, just in case they find out that we managed to avoid leaving our delicious, charcoal-broiled selves at the house."

Sam pushed a branch aside. "It was sure handy of you to have that tunnel. Were you expecting someone to burn down the house?"

"No, I was just bored and thought it might come in handy some day. I used to hide down there when my closest neighbor, Joco Vanhet, would come to visit."

"Bad company?"

Rigby shook his head. "The man never took a bath. I mean never. And his breath! I think all he ever ate was dogs that had been dead already for a long time."

Sam put a hand to his stomach and groaned.

"You can't fool me, kid. There's no way you can throw up until you get some food in your system. Care to take a breakfast break?"

"You have food?"

Rigby stared at Sam. "Do I have food? Now why in the world would I need to carry food, when the wonderful world of nature provides us with a delicious variety of delicacies guaranteed to satisfy any palate?"

"You going to snare a rabbit or something?"

"No time, no time. Besides, rabbits are too cute to eat. No, this morning it's the three B's. Bark, berries, and boots. Actually, that last one is "roots," but then it wouldn't be the three B's."

And so, Sam reluctantly—and Rigby enthusiastically—downed a nutritious, if rather woodsy, breakfast. Then, sooner than Sam would have liked, they were moving again.

Their general plan was to head north in order to find King Olive, free him, and return him to his rightful throne, but there were a few problems. First, they had no idea where King Olive was being held. Rigby thought that he had heard of the Boneman character and was reasonably sure that his castle was in the country of Wolfore. If not, then it was almost certainly somewhere in Cogbat, or

Rextaw. The odds were against it being in Ullop, but it couldn't be ruled out entirely.

In other words, they were proceeding in the hope that things would become more clear along the way.

In the tunnel the night before, Sam had suggested that they go to members of the Royal Guard who were still loyal to Olive.

"Nice try, junior," Rigby had said. "How would you know which are loyal? No way of telling for sure. Also, even if we got help and tried to raise a stink, who's to say that Boonder's men couldn't put a quick and bloody stop to it? And we sure wouldn't have the support of the people without Olive. After all, who are we? A grubby wet-nosed farm boy and a Royal Guard reject. No, I think the only way is for us to do this alone."

"You don't seem disappointed," Sam had whispered in the dark.

"I'm not," Rigby had answered, grinning in the darkness.

*   *   *

"Milos Hatcher?"

Milos turned from the cow he was milking, and faced a thickly-built man wearing a black tunic. "That's me," he said, standing and wiping his hands on a rag.

"I am Captain Sarbak of the King's Elite."

"The Royal Guard?"

"No. The newly formed King's Elite. I have some bad

news about your son."

The rag fell from Milos' hands. "Sam?"

"He died last night in a fire at the home of one Rigby Skeet. Mr. Skeet was also killed."

Milos felt a great coldness come over him. He stumbled against the side of the barn, gripping the wall.

Sarbak cleared his throat. "I must return to the King. I'm sorry about your son."

Milos could not respond. He vaguely heard Sarbak explaining a few of the details of the fire, but most of all he heard a continuous roar in his ears. If Sam was dead, wasn't it his own fault for sending him away?

*   *   *

It was late afternoon when Rigby and Sam stopped again.

"Thank God," Sam gasped, "I'm beat."

Rigby plopped down beside him under a tree. "Thank God and your leader, Rigby Skeet."

Sam closed his eyes, happier than he had ever been to feel the grass beneath him and the cool breeze dancing over his face.

"Don't doze off yet," said Rigby. "It's time for school."

"School?"

Rigby lightly slapped his face. "Hey! What did you come to me for, boy? To learn the manly arts of killing and all that."

Sam groaned. "I'd forgotten."

Rigby slapped him again. "Swine! Rule number one is

that you must have a good memory."

Sam sat up straight. "Hit me again and I'm going to pop you one back."

"Good! That's rule number two. If someone hits you, hit them back. But seriously, do you know what the rules of swordfighting are?"

Sam scratched his head. "Frankly, I have no idea."

Rigby laughed. "Good! There are no rules in a swordfight. There are so many stupid soldiers in this world who think you've got to follow a certain etiquette, certain battle courtesies, like never attack at night, always fight fair, if your opponent drops his sword, you pick it up and hand it to him. Idiots! The worst epitaph in the world is, well, he's dead, but he sure fought fair."

Sam nodded. "Just kill, kill, kill, huh?"

"Sure. If someone's trying to kill you, there's no reason to be nice to him. Social niceties are usually wasted on ruthless assassins. However, rocks and bricks, biting, scratching, and kicking often make quite an impression."

Rigby went on to teach Sam a few essentials about the broadsword (messy but effective), the bow and arrow (poison on the tip helps if you're not a great marksman), and the knife (direct and to the point). He discussed the all-important element of surprise, how to bluff if you're against a wall, and how to die gracefully if it got to that. He also showed Sam how to make both bow and arrow, finding the right kind of wood, cutting it, testing it. He reviewed what plants were edible and what animals were the easiest to catch. They set up a trap and quickly caught a plump squirrel.

They risked making a small fire to cook their catch, and drank from a stream just down a short ravine. They also ate more bark, and Sam realized with a jolt that it tasted good.

Afterwards, they lay back and relaxed. The fire was only glowing embers.

"What now?" asked Sam.

Rigby belched. "Well, I figure we rest another couple of hours until dark. Then we make our way back to the main road."

Sam sighed weakly. "And walk all night, huh?"

"Wrong, squirrel-breath," Rigby said gruffly. "We'll steal some horses."

Swords For Hire

THE KING

THE BOY

THE ODDBALL

THE NOTE

PART 5 **THE MAIDEN**

TWELVE

King Boonder stared at the golden worm and was bored.

Oh, the worm was realistic, all right. Larger than life, twisting in a wormlike way, it sat on a shining golden base. It was probably the finest single piece of work that the royal jeweler had ever crafted.

But Boonder was bored! He had been bored ever since Sarbak had killed the man who carried Olive's message, thwarting the true king's only chance for escape.

Maybe it would be different if Boonder actually ran the affairs of state, but Lord Aleron did all that for him. He tried setting worms on his head, even the golden worm, but none of it inspired him. He lusted after more than worms now, more than political power; he needed . . .

A woman?

The crown fell to the floor with a clank, but Boonder didn't bother to pick it up. This revelation was too overpowering. A *woman*. Yes. Someone to share his life of royal majesty!

Actually, Boonder had had little luck with the opposite sex while growing up. The girls had often laughed at him, turning instead to the more handsome and self-assured Olive.

Olive, it was *always* Olive. The girls preferred Olive. Father preferred Olive. *God* preferred Olive!

Until now.

Now Olive was rotting somewhere in a dark cell, alone and helpless. Yes, Boonder thought, now I am the king, I hold the power! I can have anything I want, including . . .

A woman?

Yes. A woman.

*   *   *

Late that afternoon, Captain Sarbak brought twelve of Parmall's most beautiful young women for presentation to the king.

Boonder sat on his throne and looked them over carefully. This was not a decision to be made lightly. After all, one does not pick a bride every day. "You," he said to the one on the far left, "take off your coat so I can see you."

The girl's eyes widened but she didn't move.

Boonder leaned forward. "Go ahead, take it off!"

The girl seemed paralyzed with fear. Sarbak stepped in and clopped her on the head with the butt of his sword. She fell limply to the floor.

"Do what the King says!" Sarbak screamed at the fallen girl.

"Sarbak," said Boonder tiredly as he rubbed his head, "don't hit the girls."

Sarbak looked skeptical, but stepped back.

The next girl was smiling a very tight smile. "All right," Boonder said, "Open the mouth and let's see the teeth."

She did.

"Eh . . . " said Boonder, "You can go."

And so it went. Boonder examined each girl in turn,

asking questions and observing closely. Some, like the girl with the bad teeth or the one with the slight concussion, were told to leave. Others remained on display for further judgment.

Most of the girls seemed very willing to marry a king. He recognized the look in their eyes as greed—as well he should, since he saw it each morning in the mirror. It wasn't until he reached the last girl in line that he met with any difficulty.

"All right," Boonder said, "What is your . . ."

"You have no right to hold me here."

Boonder looked up. "What?"

The girl continued angrily, "I was forcibly removed from my home by a ruffian in black. Let me go now. I would never marry you."

Boonder looked at the girl more closely. She was young, not older than twenty. Her auburn hair was long, and curled around her shoulders. Pretty, with a nice figure, but she wasn't dressed up like the other girls. No, this girl was more of a diamond in the rough.

And those eyes! Boonder sensed that she felt only contempt for him.

He knew that he must have her.

He smiled and clutched the golden worm in his left hand without thinking. "I choose you. The rest may leave!"

The girl cried in anger. "You slimy, greasy monster! You have no right to do this! I hate you!"

Sarbak quickly stepped forward, his sword raised. "Don't talk like that, missy," he said in a threatening voice.

"No, Sarbak!" Boonder barked. The King and Sarbak stared at each other. "You may leave now," said Boonder quietly, "And take these stragglers with you. You can do with them as you like."

Sarbak grinned then, a horrible grin. "Yes, sir."

When the rest had left, Boonder turned to the girl. "What is your name?"

The girl looked up, slowly, defiantly. "I will not answer your questions, I will not play along with your perverted games, I will not marry you. I wish to see my father."

Boonder stood and approached the girl. "Your father will be paid. As for you, you will stay here with me."

"You filth," she said coldly, "what gives you the right . . ."

The last word was hardly out before Boonder's hand lashed out in a cruel slap, knocking her to the ground. He was breathing hard and smiling. The girl sobbed softly, and did not look up.

It was then that Boonder realized why he wanted this particular girl instead of one of the others. The others would have married him to share his wealth, his power, his prestige. But the girls Boonder always wanted were the ones he couldn't have. The ones who laughed at him, joked about his worms, called him grease-head—those were the girls he wanted to take, to show them what a man he was. That was why he had to have . . .

"What is your name?" he demanded again.

The girl propped herself up on one arm. "Melinda," she said, spitting. "What's yours?"

Boonder threw back his head and let out a deep,

hysterical laugh. He turned back to the girl, his palms beginning to sweat. Melinda might indeed hate him now.

But she would learn to love him.

THIRTEEN

Days passed, and their journey northward continued. Now that they had horses, Rigby and Sam were making much better time. The only drawback was that the horses made it difficult to move off the road in a hurry if people approached. Twice they had been almost caught by the owner of the horses and his friends.

They continued to travel mostly at night. Each day, with the coming of dawn, they had to find a cave or another hidden place to camp. They were always careful to leave the horses elsewhere, sometimes half a mile away.

"Is that the sun I see?" Sam asked one morning. It had been six days since Rigby's shack had burned.

"I expect so," nodded Rigby, pulling his cloak tighter around him. "And not a minute too soon. Thought I'd freeze my butt off last night." Rigby's horse stepped in rhythm under him.

"Yeah," Sam agreed. "A pity Olive couldn't have been taken to a Southern jail."

"Ah," sighed Rigby wistfully. "Have you ever been to sunny Kampo Vista?"

Sam coughed. "I've heard stories."

"They're all true. Such women down there! You wouldn't believe it. Your eyes would pop out of your head and you would die. But I swear—they move like snakes, gently swaying to the rhythm. And the wine! Nectar kissed by the sun . . . What a great time I had."

"Really nice, huh?"

"You bet. They put me in jail for over a year."

Sam began to slip off his horse, but straightened himself. "What in the world did you do?"

Rigby laughed, then spat. "You don't want to hear it. Besides, I don't want to ruin any tender illusions you may still have about my integrity and character. Anyway, what I did isn't considered as bad as horse stealing."

Sam looked down at his horse uneasily. "No?"

"No. For horse stealing they hang you. Sometimes they cut off your ears, hands, or nose first, though."

"I trust this happens only in Kampo Vista?"

Rigby tapped at his half-frozen beard. "No, I'm afraid that's universal law."

A week ago Sam might have fainted but this morning he laughed. With a tug on the reins he moved closer, then kicked Rigby hard in the leg.

"Ow!" said Rigby. "What's with you, farm boy?"

Sam urged his horse forward. "I can kick you anytime I want," said Sam. "Universal law."

Now the sun was clearly visible, and they realized they had to find shelter soon. They left the main road and began to move through the thick woods.

"Cave, I think," Sam said shortly.

"Where?"

"Through the trees to the right."

As they made their way through the trees, they saw that it was indeed a cave. When they reached it, Rigby dismounted. "Well, this is near perfect," he said. "Big enough for us and the horses, and pretty well hidden by the trees, too."

They circled back to a nearby creek to water the horses and get water for themselves as well. Then they returned to the cave, taking the horses with them.

The cave was cool and damp. Sam strained to look but could not see how far the cave receded back into the darkness.

Rigby leaned against the cave wall and sighed. "A fine thing," he said. "We freeze all night and then don't even get to see the sun in the daytime."

Sam eased himself down near Rigby. Sam's legs were simply not used to such constant riding. "What's for dinner?" he asked.

Rigby rummaged though a leather knapsack. "We've still got quite a bit left from the things we stole: bread, a little cheese, some dried beef . . ."

"*Intruders!*" A voice rang out behind them.

Rigby shook his head. "No, no intruders. We must have eaten the last of the intruders yesterday."

"You are intruders in this cave! You must leave!"

Rigby looked toward the cave entrance where Sam was already staring. There stood a bald man in an ornate cloak.

Rigby rose. "Hi. Rigby Skeet, sword for hire. And this is my partner, the slow, yet innocent Sam Hatcher."

"You will come with me," the bald man said. "The master will want to see you."

Sam looked at Rigby anxiously. What was going on? But Rigby's face was blank.

"You heard the man, Sam-boy. Let's see where he takes us."

The bald man bowed slightly and walked farther back into the cave. Rigby followed casually, but Sam noticed that his hand was resting lightly on his sword grip. Sam swallowed, touched the knife at his side, and followed into the darkness.

The path led deep into the cave, then down. They passed two torches along the way, but they provided very little light against the overwhelming darkness. Finally, just as Sam thought he might scream from claustrophobia, the dark tunnel emptied into a vast, well-lit opening.

"The chamber of the great Sirca Long," the bald man said, motioning them inside.

"Heavenly days and night," said Rigby softly.

"Wow," agreed Sam.

The chamber was huge. The uneven rocky walls were covered by fine tapestries, and large lanterns hung high on the walls, brightly lighting the entire area. The furniture was elegant: gold-encrusted tables, finely-crafted footstools, and chairs adorned with jewels. But the focus of this setting was the figure sitting in a golden chair by the far wall, dressed in a simple black cloak. The man was bearded, and very old.

Rigby spoke first. "Sirca Long?"

The old man merely smiled.

Rigby turned back toward the bald man. "Doesn't he like me?"

But the bald man was gone.

Sam was getting scared—this was weird. "Rigby, where did the bald guy go?"

Rigby said nothing, but his hand gripped his sword tighter as his grey eyes scanned the cavern. Then, slowly, he began to walk toward the old man.

"R'taa!" cried the old man.

Suddenly a jet of flame leaped from the wall just inches from Rigby's face.

"Rigby!" Sam cried.

But Rigby had dived to the left, strung an arrow, and fired it at the old man. It struck four inches to the left of his head.

"The next one goes through your left eye and nails your head to the wall," Rigby hissed.

The old man leaned back and laughed. "No need for that. Pach'ula!" The flame disappeared. "Yes, I am Sirca Long."

Rigby relaxed, but only a little. "Pleased to meet you, I'm sure. Well, maybe I'm not so sure."

Sam moved next to Rigby, his knife drawn. "You okay, Rigby?"

"Yeah. Well, Sirca Long, I am Rigby Skeet, sword for hire, and this is my colleague and straight man, Sam Hatcher."

Sirca Long tugged at his white beard. "Please sit."

Sam looked at Rigby apprehensively. Sirca Long smiled. "You must forgive my unorthodox behavior. I receive so few visitors, it is difficult not to show off a bit, yes?"

A bit reluctantly, they sat.

THE KING

THE BOY

THE ODDBALL

THE NOTE

THE MAIDEN

PART 6   THE SORCERER

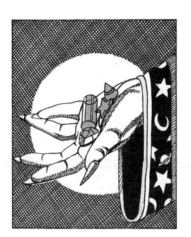

FOURTEEN

The old man folded his hands. "As Cheng probably told you, I am the greatest sorcerer in all the world, with powers that you could not dream of. I know things only the gods know, as I have lived for hundreds of years."

Rigby and Sam sat quietly. Sam wondered what Sirca Long intended.

The old man paused, then suddenly looked up with cold eyes. "Why have you invaded my domain?"

"You know, it takes a good deal to confuse me, but brother, I'm confused. You lost me with that last part. What the devil are you talking about?" Rigby said.

"You came here to steal my treasure, didn't you? My wealth is sung of far and wide! Did your dirty greed lead you here?" Sirca Long's eyes were now wide with fury.

Sam stood up. "Now wait a minute. I was just a farmer's boy until a couple of weeks ago, and now Rigby and I are on our way to save King Olive. We entered your cave for shelter, didn't know anything about any treasure, just wanted to sleep for a little bit, that's all. Can we leave now?"

Sirca Long seemed to soften. He continued to question the pair but without the same intensity. Finally, after what seemed like an hour, he seemed satisfied. His animosity left him, and the two adventurers were invited to a sumptuous repast.

They sat around a gold-encrusted table and were served by Cheng, the bald man.

Sam shoveled food into his mouth, ignoring manners in his hunger. Rigby ate more neatly, but with equal speed. Sirca Long ate slowly, smiling at their ferocious attack upon the meal.

After several minutes, Rigby paused, took a long draught of wine, and said, "By the bye, have you ever heard of a character called the Boneman?"

Sirca Long's fork fell from his hand, his face white with fear. "The Boneman?"

Rigby nodded. "That's the guy who's keeping our king prisoner. Heard of him?"

The old man wiped a hand over his face. "Yes . . . yes, of course, I have heard stories." He closed his eyes and clenched his fists tightly. "If you value your lives, do not seek him out. He is death incarnate."

Sam suddenly felt his appetite leave him. Rigby looked at him and smiled. "Don't worry, Sam-boy. I met this other guy once who was supposed to be death incarnate." He smiled sheepishly. "He *was* when I got through with him."

Sirca Long stood up, quivering. "You may joke now in the safety of my holy abode," he warned, "but when you confront him, there will be no jokes. There will only be death."

Sam and Rigby finished their meals in silence. The old man then reached inside a drawer and brought forth two objects. "Gifts," he said, "from Sirca Long, master sorcerer, to aid you on your journey."

He turned to Sam and handed him a small green rock.

"The Stone of Alastar," he said. "Keep it with you at all times and it shall give you courage to face your enemies."

"Thank you," said Sam, holding the stone carefully.

"And Rigby Skeet," Sirca Long said, "I present you the Rod of Ulluwine. If you raise it in your hand, it shall always tug on you and show the correct path to take."

"Thanks," said Rigby, taking the small clear cylinder.

"But I warn you," said Sirca Long, "if the rod should ever break, you shall surely die."

Rigby cleared his throat. "Yeah, thanks a lot. I couldn't just take some beads instead, could I?"

"Enough!" cried the old man. "I have fed you, and given you gifts. My last gift is this," he added, drawing a folded piece of paper from a small jeweled chest. "A map that will take you to the Boneman."

Suddenly Cheng appeared again. "Time for you to leave," he said.

Rigby bowed slightly. "Thanks for your help."

"Do not thank me," Sirca Long said coldly. "I am sending you to your deaths."

Without another word, Cheng led them back to the cave entrance. As they approached the opening, Rigby turned and noticed that Cheng had again disappeared.

"Gone again," Rigby said. "Was it something we said?"

Sam shook his head in bewilderment. "Come on, Sword for Hire, let's find a nice normal cave with rats and snakes and bats."

A few hours later, after a not-entirely successful attempt at rest, the two adventurers were on the move once more, their horses moving steadily under a full moon.

Sam fingered the magical stone in his pocket. "It's really a lucky thing that we happened to stop in that cave," he said thoughtfully. "Not only do we have a map to lead us to the Boneman, but now this stone will give me the courage to face him."

Rigby made a farting sound with his mouth and kept on riding.

"What's with you?" Sam demanded. "That guy was a sorcerer!"

Rigby spat. "And I'm a blind chipmunk."

Sam rode on in stubborn silence.

Two hours later Sam said, "You really think he was a fake?"

Rigby nodded. "I don't want to trample your dreams, kid, and if you want to leap into the fray holding that piece of rock in front of you, you just be my guest."

"But what about that burst of flame? And all those riches?"

"Trickery," Rigby answered. "I can't tell you exactly how he did the fire bit, but that treasure was less than it appeared. See this under my fingernail?"

Sam squinted. "Ah, it's hard in this light . . . something shiny?"

Rigby smiled. "Some of the gold inlay on that table. It's paint. Just paint."

Again, Sam fell silent. Finally he said, "What about your magic rod?"

Rigby reached into his pocket. "A friendly gesture on

the old guy's part, I suppose, but it's still superstitious nonsense."

"Hey! Careful with that! He said if you break it, you . . ."

"I will surely die," said Rigby. "Like *this*." Rigby snapped the rod in two.

"RIGBY!"

But Rigby couldn't answer. He was coughing violently and clutching at his chest. Sam leaped from his horse and landed next to Rigby's. Rigby was now still, slumped forward on the horse. Drool ran from his open mouth.

With strength he never dreamed he possessed, Sam lifted his friend from the horse and set him gently on the ground.

"Rigby?" Sam said quietly, probing for signs of life. Pulse? Heartbeat? Frustrated beyond belief, Sam couldn't find them. Breath? He put a hand in front of Rigby's nose, and waited for tense seconds. Nothing. And then, a slight, warm whiff of air.

He was breathing!

Sam rushed back to the horse to get some wine to try to revive Rigby. The wine sack seemed lost in the pouch of provisions, but Sam kept digging, throwing things on the ground, until he finally gripped the wineskin. He turned to take it to his dying friend, his only friend in this strange land, his . . .

Rigby was standing right behind him, smiling. "I guess that curse didn't work after all. By the way, I prefer my wine chilled."

Sam's fist caught Rigby square in the jaw and his eyes

widened in rage. "You rotten freak!" he said, "You dirty, rotten freak!"

Rigby had picked himself up and was nursing his jaw, but he was smiling. "Good lad!" he cried. "The fist, that's what's real! The right to the jaw, the sword to the gut! Not that magical junk!"

Sam's fists were still clenched, but his eyes softened a little.

"This is lesson number forty-three in a series," Rigby said, brushing himself off. "Collect them all."

They got on their horses without another word. Rigby still had a smile on his face and Sam a scowl on his.

But as they rode on, Rigby noticed that Sam took the magic stone from his pocket and hurled it far into the darkness.

FIFTEEN

King Boonder awoke with a scream.

Within seconds a black-garbed member of the King's Elite burst into the room. "Your Majesty," the man said, "are you all right?"

Boonder was sitting up in bed, sweating. "Yes," he said, panting.

The guard's sword was drawn. "Didn't I hear a scream?"

Boonder nodded. "I . . . I had the most horrid dream. I dreamed that . . . my brother Olive came back . . . and took the throne away from me. He took all my power! I wasn't king anymore!"

The guard shook his head in disgust. If this greasy mongrel didn't pay so well . . . "Don't let it bother you, sir," he said with barely-hidden contempt. "Only a dream."

Boonder reached over to his bedside table and clutched the golden worm tightly, stroking it to calm himself. "Yes," he said, "only a dream."

The guard stood for a moment, watching the ruler of Parmall fondle a golden worm. Finally he said, "Will that be all?"

Boonder looked up. Sweat was still streaming from his face. "Yes, yes, that's all."

The guard nodded. "Get some sleep, Your Majesty. It's still the middle of the night."

"Yes," King Boonder said as the guard closed the door. "I will."

But he didn't.

In the morning, as Boonder finished his breakfast, he looked toward Melinda, who sat before her untouched plate. "It's the day of our wedding, my dear."

Melinda sat very still, head down. She had learned from experience that insolence was rewarded with pain.

Boonder leaned close to her, and she could smell his sweat. "Give us a smile," he said.

There was no choice. She smiled, and felt herself dying inside.

Boonder grinned. "That's a girl, Melinda." He was very proud of the job he had done with her. Why, at first, she had spat on him and called him all manner of vile names. But just look at her now . . .

Melinda looked up at the King of Parmall through her long auburn hair. Her eyes were red from crying. "Please do not force me to marry you," she pleaded. "In the name of all that's holy—"

Boonder slapped her hard, his royal ring making a red indentation on her cheek. "We've been all through this," he said quietly, "and I don't want to hear any more argument. All right?"

It was a nightmare. What could she say? "All right."

"That's it. Now I wanted to mention one more thing before the ceremony. If at any time you try to create a disturbance or indicate that you don't wish to marry me, I shall have your father killed. Understand?"

"Perfectly."

"Good. And then, after the ceremony, we shall return to my royal chambers."

Her face was white with rage.

"And if there is any disturbance there," Boonder said with a grin, "I shall put you in the tender care of my Elite guards." His eyes were like burning coals.

Melinda closed her eyes. "I understand perfectly."

"For your sake," said Boonder, "I hope that you do."

*   *   *

The wedding ceremony was thankfully brief. King Boonder led the procession wearing an outlandish light-blue silk robe with embroidered frills and bright gold trim around the edges. On his head he wore brightly-colored hoonu feathers around his crown. Lord Aleron had advised Boonder to wear traditional dress, but Boonder knew that as king, his own judgement was better.

That logic also led Boonder to dress his bride-to-be in a plain, coarse peasant dress. "Until she marries me, she's a peasant," he had reasoned. "She will wear finery only when she becomes my queen." Boonder nodded to himself, appreciating the symbolism.

An enormous crowd had gathered for this nuptial farce. Peasants, farmers, and shopkeepers left their homes for miles around to get a glimpse of the new queen—a peasant girl at that! Actually, the only ones not present at the ceremony were the thieves and robbers who were finding the many empty homes quite attractive pickings.

The palace priest was an old man who turned the pages of the holy book with trembling fingers. As the bride and groom approached him, a silence fell over the crowd, and the wedding began.

"Holy the first. Praise the name of the Lord everlasting here and forever, amen," the priest mumbled.

Melinda looked ahead blankly, as Boonder rubbed his palms together.

"Holy the second. Thanks be for the soil, from which cometh the food we eat, amen."

The crowd watched eagerly, heads straining for a better view. The priest paused, fumbling as he turned a page, and then continued.

"Holy the third. None shall eat the meat of the quekle nor the fruit of the bossa tree, on pain of death, amen."

Boonder's hands were sweating as he rubbed them tightly together. Until now, he had forgotten that the Parmall wedding service always began with a reading of the forty Holy Orders.

"Holy the fourth. None but the high priest may enter the chamber of communion from which the Lord delivers his holy word."

The veins were standing out on Boonder's temples.

"Holy the fifth. The lights in the night sky shall be revered—"

Boonder closed his eyes, his anger building.

Lord Aleron stepped forward and whispered into the priest's ear. "If you desire to live through this day, you should very quickly learn to count by tens."

The old man's eyes grew wide with fear, and for a moment he was silent. Quiet mumblings could be heard from the crowd.

The priest swallowed, then continued with a much-shortened ceremony. The royal wedding was over before most of the crowd was aware that it had once again started.

King Boonder and the peasant girl Melinda were now officially married. The king smiled in vicious triumph, as the queen began to look for a way to take her own life.

SIXTEEN

Melinda sat on the bed, unable to cry. There were no tears left. There was nothing left, only life with an abominable pig.

She had already searched the room for a weapon with which to kill herself. She knew that she dare not attempt to assassinate the king for fear of what would happen to her family. But her search was useless. The only possible method that she could see was to hang herself with a silken bedsash tied to one of the high bedposts. But when she tried this, one of the King's Elite came in and stopped her. She was being watched, then. Melinda wondered with revulsion if they kept watch at all hours.

The King entered, sliding the bolt in the door behind him. He looked at her and smiled—the smile of a starving man about to devour a piece of meat. His eyes glowed. "Come here," he ordered.

Melinda stood, very slowly.

Boonder was ecstatic. Power, he thought, that's the key. To be in total control, total command of any situation. I'm in total command of this country. I'm in total control of this woman.

Melinda stood motionless.

"Come here!" he repeated.

Melinda hesitated. Refusal meant being thrown to the barbaric Elite Guard, and death and pain to her family. There were no choices, only darkness everywhere. Her vision blurred, and she felt dizzy and nauseous. If only someone could save me, she thought.

"Now!" Boonder snarled. He crouched like an animal about to pounce.

Melinda was vaguely aware that she was slowly stepping toward Boonder.

He smiled. What the king wants, the king gets.

There was a sudden pounding at the door.

"Begone!" Boonder shrieked.

"I must have words with you, Sire!" It was Captain Sarbak's voice.

Boonder paused, his face crimson with anger. "You fool! I am busy, now begone!"

"You must listen to me, Sire—"

"The devil if I will!" Boonder faced the bolted door, his fists clenched. "Leave me alone and do not bother me again!"

There was silence from the other side of the door, then Boonder heard Sarbak quietly say, "It's about your brother."

Boonder seemed to collapse like a leaky balloon. His regal power, his total control, all gone. He weakly unbolted the door.

Sarbak entered. "Remember the two men we burned up in that house because they might have gotten Olive's message?"

Boonder's head was already spinning. "Yes?"

"Well, I don't think they're dead."

Boonder began to shiver and chew on his lip. "Not dead? But—but how? Oh, they've just got to be dead!"

Captain Sarbak explained how one of his men had decided to dig through the rubble and see if anything of value had survived the fire. As he searched, he noticed that there were no human remains. This had led to a more thorough search, which turned up a tunnel leading out of the house.

"So our guess is they made it out," Sarbak said. "Whether they went to find Olive or are still in this country, it's up for grabs. They may not have even got the message about Olive."

"No," Boonder said, almost crying, "I know they got it. They want to take all this away from me."

"Any orders, Majesty?"

Boonder looked up. "What are the men's names?"

"Rigby Skeet and Sam Hatcher, Sire. They sound harmless enough."

"They are guilty of treason against the king and the state. They are to be killed on sight. Put posters around the kingdom proclaiming that." Boonder had sunk into a large chair, and was curling himself into a tight ball. "Also, double the palace guards. That will be all."

"Good night, Majesty," said Sarbak with a slimy smile. "Happy honeymoon."

The door closed, and the king remained in the chair.

Melinda watched him from across the room, absorbing what she had heard.

Boonder reached to the table and grasped the golden worm. He stroked it anxiously, shutting his eyes and making little mewing sounds.

And as she watched, Melinda realized that as long as the two men, Skeet and Hatcher, were on the loose, she would be free from the king's pawing hands. She looked at him and smiled, amazed at the smallness of the man before her. She may have only been a peasant girl, but he—he was a worm.

Melinda smiled. It felt good to smile again. She had been no more than a mannequin the past few days. Now, if anyone could have seen her, they would have seen a young woman, alive and really beautiful.

She thanked God, then she thanked Rigby Skeet and Sam Hatcher—such lovely names, she thought—then walked to the quivering mass that was king of Parmall.

"Is there anything I can do?" she asked innocently.

He waved his hand. "Oh, go away. You can sleep in the guest chamber until I need you."

"As you wish," she replied. As she closed the door, she could hear him begin to cry. It was music to her ears, and she whistled quietly all the way to the guest chambers.

The queen slept much better than the king that night.

Swords For Hire

SEVENTEEN

Sam Hatcher had once dreamed of travel. He had looked up from his pigs or grain and gazed longingly at that mysterious land just beyond the next hill. Someday he had hoped he would walk down that road and discover new people and exotic new lands.

Sam Hatcher no longer dreamed of travel. He now dreamed of a comfy chair, a decent meal, a few hours of peace and quiet. He got none of these.

"Chin up, Sam," said Rigby. "We're almost there."

The road to find the Boneman had not been an easy one. They had been forced to travel though the infamous Forest of Darkness, where Sam had been attacked by a giant, vicious . . . something.

Rigby and Sam had a long argument later about just what the thing in the dark was, but they finally decided that in some cases it was better not to know. Rigby's quick action with an arrow had sent the thing loping off into the wilderness.

Later, they had to cross the River of Blood, slosh through the Swamp of Anguish, and walk through the Pasture of Randolph.

"Pasture of Randolph?" Sam had asked.

"I guess Randolph owns it," Rigby replied.

Rigby's horse had gone lame, and Sam's refused to cross the River of Blood, so the two adventurers were traversing the last few miles on foot. They moved slowly but steadily, eyes alert for danger.

"Even if we find Olive," Sam panted, "how are we going to get him out? There must be guards and things."

Rigby removed a burr from his tangled beard. "Are you scared of the guards or the things?"

"Both."

Rigby sighed. "Well—the way I look at it, we're doing pretty well. They didn't kill us in the fire back at my late great home, we miraculously got a map leading us to the Bonefellow, and now we're almost there. I presume that some sort of incredibly brilliant plan will surface as we proceed."

Sam nodded uneasily. "I hope you're right . . . "

"Graakk!" cried Rigby suddenly as a burly man with drawn sword jumped from the tree above and landed on him.

"Rigby!" Sam cried.

The attacker was big and had caught Rigby totally unprepared. He twisted wildly under the weight as the attacker moved his sword in for the kill.

"SAM!"

Sam was frozen. He held a knife in his hand, but somehow, he couldn't move.

Rigby tried desperately to grab the man's wrists to force the blade away. The attacker lunged downward with his sword, and blood gushed from Rigby's left arm.

Sam moved now, although he felt like he was dreaming. A scream burst from his lips as he lunged toward the man. He gripped the attacker roughly from behind, grabbing his sword arm with one hand, and with the other . . .

And with the other he plunged his knife into the man's throat.

The rest was a blur; the horrible gurgling scream, the mad jumble of bodies, and the blood . . . all the blood.

From attack to finish, the battle had taken only twelve seconds.

Sam shoved the corpse to one side and Rigby stood, his tunic smeared with the dead man's blood and his arm smeared with his own. The two stared at each other.

"You waited," Rigby said, panting. "He had a sword to my neck, and you waited."

Sam could say nothing. His hands were sticky with blood.

Exhausted, Rigby eased himself back down on the ground and swallowed. "It's not like I'm sorry you saved my life. Thank you for that."

The world began to spin, and Sam felt his last meal rise. He bent over and retched. Finally the sickness passed. He straightened and stumbled down a hill to a creek. The water was cold but cleansing as it washed away the blood and the vomit. The stinging water hurt, but Sam reveled in it. It was a small way to atone for his sins.

Finally he stood up, his hands and face numb.

"We better build a fire or you're going to freeze," Rigby said as he stood behind him. Although Sam had not noticed, Rigby had washed himself also.

"Yeah," Sam said finally. "A fire."

Later, after the fire had died to glowing embers, Rigby asked, "How do you feel?"

"Okay, I guess," Sam said quietly. "Your arm okay?"

"Yeah," Rigby paused a moment. "The last thing in God's wonderful world that you need is a big lecture from me about innocent farm boys confronting death. But that big oaf with the sword tells me that we're getting within range of whatever it is we're after. It's going to get rougher, not easier, from here on out. And I gotta know, Sam—can I depend on you in the tight spots? Or are you going to freeze up on me?"

The wind rustled through the trees. "I don't know," Sam said evenly.

Rigby nodded. "An honest answer."

"Hadn't we better get moving, then?" Sam asked.

"Sure you're up to it?"

Sam smiled slightly. "I don't know."

Rigby got to his feet with a grunt. "I think I'm going to get tired of those honest answers."

*　　*　　*

Imagine a dark, sinister-looking castle, then multiply by two and you'd have the castle of the Boneman.

"Yikes," Sam whispered.

"Double yikes with gravy," whispered back Rigby.

It truly was a nasty looking place. Huge dark turrets rose from somber castle walls. A moat, black as ink, surrounded it. In the moat, dark, powerful forms slithered about. Guards were stationed at the gate, and archers manned many of the windows and parapets.

"Let's go home now," Rigby said.

"Okay," said Sam.

"I just remembered, I don't have a home to go home to."

Sam nodded. "That's right. Then I guess we might as well get ourselves killed trying to free King Olive."

Rigby stroked his dark beard. "Okay."

They crouched low in their hiding place, some distance from the castle.

"Sam," Rigby said, "you run up to the main gate there and ask if King Olive can come out to play. If he can, fine. If not, you pull your sword and start hacking your way through the guards. I'll stay here and grade your performance."

"I've got a better idea," replied Sam. "You go up to the main gate and tell them that you're the legendary Rigby Skeet, sword for hire. The guards will either run in terror or drop dead of fear."

Rigby shook his head. "Good thinking, but what if they speak a different language up here? They might think I said I was Rigby Skeet, world champion spitter. Then they'd throw me in the moat."

Sam grinned but swallowed hard. "Rigby, what are we going to do?"

Rigby smiled. "Thought you'd never ask."

Rigby prided himself on his battle strategy. He liked to think that he had a quick, inventive mind. And, in fact, he did.

Who else in the world could devise a plan to get *into* the Boneman's castle?

THE KING

THE BOY

THE ODDBALL

THE NOTE

THE MAIDEN

THE SORCERER

PART 7   **THE BONEMAN**

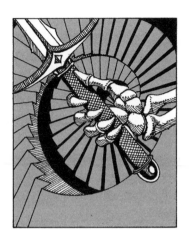

EIGHTEEN

By pretending Sam was a prisoner King Boonder wanted imprisoned, Rigby and Sam easily passed the main guard station at the castle gate.

"Move along, whelp!" growled Rigby, pushing Sam against the rough stone wall.

"I tell you I am innocent!" cried Sam.

The guard who was leading them inside looked back at Rigby and grinned. "They all say that."

He took them down a long dark corridor which led to the office of the Dungeon Keeper.

The Dungeon Keeper sat behind a desk in the center of the room. One wall was covered with keys, the others lined with tall bookshelves. Books and papers were stacked everywhere. The old man coughed and looked up. "Yes?"

"A new prisoner," the guard said. "From King Boonder."

The old man jerked his head up. "That's impossible! I have no such message from Boonder. In fact, his last stated that there might be two rebels on their way to . . ."

Sam's fist caught the old gentleman squarely in the jaw. He fell backward with a grunt. The ropes that had bound Sam had fallen to the floor. Rigby was also moving. His elbow plunged deep into the guard's stomach, and another solid punch sent the guard against a stone wall. His head hit hard, and he collapsed.

The old man and the guard lay unconscious.

"I can't believe how easy this is," Rigby said, shaking his head in disbelief.

"Come on," Sam said, "help me tie them up."

Moments later, wearing the clothes of the downed guards, Sam and Rigby began to scour the walls, looking for the right key.

"We'll never find it," Sam said, "there are hundreds."

"Have faith, boy, faith," said Rigby, his eyes scanning the keys.

"Good Lord," Sam said softly.

"What is it?"

Sam whistled quietly. "This key. It's labeled 'Olive.'"

Rigby walked toward Sam. "You're kidding."

Sam pointed. "See? Right there. Cell 001, it says."

Rigby shook his head. "It's a good thing you found it and not me. I can't read, remember?"

"Yeah, but just as soon as we get out of here I'm going to teach you."

Rigby grabbed the key and shook his head. "I can't believe how easy this is."

Sam picked up a guard's sword and slipped it alongside his own, then the two men began to move down the dark corridor. They passed several guards, but a mumbled salute seemed to get them past without any problems.

And then they came to the stairs. Not just stairs. *The stairs.*

They seemed endless. Rigby and Sam trudged down several flights and emerged at a corridor with cells on both sides, but all the numbers were too high.

"No," Rigby said, "he must be farther down."

So they went farther down. And down. At each landing

they stopped, hoping they had reached King Olive, but each time they had to return to the dimly-lit stairs and proceed downward once more.

As they trudged downward, Sam said, "Rigby, what do you think about this Boneman guy? Sirca Long was scared to death of him. And even his own guards seem petrified just being here."

"Shut up and trudge," Rigby panted.

"But Rigby," Sam persisted, "do you think he's really just made out of bones, or what?"

Rigby paused, resting against the stone wall. "Look, Sam, I'm made out of bones and you're made out of bones. So what? Ducks are made out of bones! Fish are made out of bones! Weasels . . ."

Sam sighed. "We better keep moving, I guess."

Rigby grunted. "Yeah."

And they kept going down. And down. And down. Their breath became ragged and their legs felt like rotted wood, but still they went down. And down. And down. Until they couldn't go any farther. Then they stopped.

"End of the line," said Rigby.

"He's got to be here," Sam whispered back.

The light was almost nonexistent in this corridor. Rigby drew his single torch from his pouch and lit it. There was only one door, at the far end of the corridor. Above it was a number: 001.

"That's it," Sam whispered.

They moved quietly to the cell door. It was made of thick metal, with only a tiny window near the top. Rigby put his eye to it.

"Can't see a thing," he whispered. "We might as well go ahead and open it."

Rigby took the key from his pocket. At first he thought it didn't fit, but after some jiggling the rusty lock turned and the door opened. Rigby stepped inside, holding the torch high. In a corner of the cell was a hairy manacled man in torn clothing. The man held out his filthy hand to shield his eyes from the light of the torch.

Sam moved beside Rigby, staring at this thing that was once a man.

Rigby was the first to speak. "King Olive?"

"Do not mock me," the man rasped. "My precious brother is the king now."

Sam's eyes grew wide. "Then you *are* King Olive?"

"I was," the man said coldly. "What do you men want?"

Sam stepped forward. "We've come to free you, Your Majesty."

The manacles were a problem, although not an insurmountable one. Rigby and Sam had brought files and a saw. As they worked, Rigby told Olive the story of his rescue and of his rescuers. Finally, Olive was free.

He stood, rubbing his wrists. How long had it has been since I could lift an arm without pulling along a length of chain, he wondered. Sam handed him the guard's sword he had brought.

Rigby sat in a corner, resting for a moment. "I can't believe how easy this is. Frankly, King Olive, I never thought we'd find you."

Standing and stretching, raising his new sword high, the dishevelled prisoner somehow looked regal. "Yes, and I hoped against hope that someone would receive my message. You two are indeed sent from God."

Sam stood. "Well, we'd better get moving if . . ."

THUMP.

"What was that?" asked Rigby.

THUMP.

Olive's face turned pale. "He's coming."

THUMP.

"Who's coming?" Sam asked.

THUMP.

King Olive shivered involuntarily. "The Boneman."

THUMP.

Rigby opened his mouth to say something, but then didn't. There was nothing to say. He had been right, really. It *was* incredibly easy to get inside the castle of the Boneman.

The hard part was getting out.

NINETEEN

The Boneman was coming.

King Olive felt his dreams of freedom wither within his breast.

Suddenly a hideous shrieking laugh burst forth from the corridor. It sounded like nothing that could come from a human.

"Well," Rigby said quietly, "at least he has a sense of humor."

The heavy clanking, shambling noise moved closer. *"My dear Olive,"* rasped the chilling voice, *"you should know there is no escape from the Boneman."*

There was silence for a moment, and Sam felt his heart pounding in his chest.

All three men flinched when the Boneman suddenly shrieked, *"Guards!"*

From inside the cell, Rigby, Sam, and the King could hear dozens of footsteps cascading down the stairway.

"Listen," Rigby said, "I don't like this situation any more than you guys, but what say we step outside this cell and size up the competition?"

"They'll kill us," Sam whispered.

"Better that than being locked in here," King Olive said. "Believe me."

And so, swords drawn, the three men stepped into the corridor. Sam swallowed. "May God help us."

Standing about twenty feet away from them was the Boneman. *"I am the only god here, fool."*

Olive swallowed hard and closed his eyes. The Boneman was, if anything, far worse than he had ever imagined.

Taller than any man Olive had ever seen, he wore a long black cape and hood, so that the only visible parts of his body were his face and hands. And those . . . those were the face and hands of a skeleton. A living, moving skeleton. Rigby peered closer and saw that it was no mask, no trick of the light. The Boneman was truly something inhuman.

Behind him now were perhaps twenty armed guards, completely blocking the stairway.

"Okay," Rigby said to Sam. "I'll take the one on the left, and you handle the rest of them."

Sam was in no mood for jokes. "Rigby, what are we going to do?"

"Die," the Boneman answered, his skull-face grinning broadly. *"You and your friend will die. But Olive will merely suffer. He will suffer for all eternity."*

Suddenly Olive felt all fear vanish, pushed out by an even more overwhelming rush of anger. And indignation. And hate.

"You monster," he said, stepping forward with sword in hand. "You vile monster." His eyes grew fiery, his gaze strong. "First my kingdom is taken from me. Then you chain me in a dark cell for *years,* letting me suffer alone in the darkness, feeding me filth, crushing my spirit . . . You took my life away." He gripped his sword tighter. "And now I'll do the same to you."

"No doubt you will try," said the Boneman, cackling.

"Come on, Rigby," said Sam, "let's all rush him at once."

"Guards," the Boneman said, *"if the other two make the slightest movement during my battle with Olive—kill them."*

A dozen arrows were aimed at Rigby and Sam.

"You see," the Boneman explained with a voice from the grave, *"I prefer doing this one at a time. First I will maim, and perhaps cripple, King Olive. He will then be placed back in his cell for all eternity. And then, since I have no use for the two of you, I shall kill you. Most unpleasantly, I assure you."*

Rigby and Sam exchanged glances.

"I guess it's a good thing you taught me the part about dying gracefully," Sam said.

"Sorry, kid," Rigby said, swallowing hard. "About everything."

The Boneman drew out a long, heavy sword. His tall frame seemed to tower over everyone else. *"It's time, Olive. Now I punish you for your indiscretions."*

Olive moved closer, holding the sword in front of him.

The Boneman gave a hideous laugh. *"You make the pretense of fighting me with that sword. But I know that your arms have almost atrophied from lack of use!"*

You're wrong, Olive thought. You don't know that I spent every moment in that pit exercising and pulling against the chains. My arms and legs are thick and strong, Boneman.

The man and the thing moved closer together.

"I can't watch," said Sam, but he did anyway.

"*Over three years in that cell,*" the Boneman rasped. "*You are weak, Olive.*"

Olive said nothing. He moved closer to his captor, looking for an opening. Olive was short, and the Boneman towered more than two feet above him. Still, Olive showed no sign of fear.

"*I have never been defeated,*" croaked the Boneman. "*I will make you feel such exquisite pain.*"

And then Olive, for reasons even he couldn't explain, smiled.

The Boneman drew back involuntarily, but then, with a shriek, he lunged forward with his huge, deadly sword.

At the last possible instant, Olive deflected the blow harmlessly aside.

An inhuman bellow came from the Boneman as he lunged again. This time Olive stepped under the sword thrust and with a quick upward motion, chopped the Boneman's sword hand off at the wrist.

Swords For Hire

THE KING

THE BOY

THE ODDBALL

THE NOTE

THE MAIDEN

THE SORCERER

THE BONEMAN

PART 8   THE ESCAPE

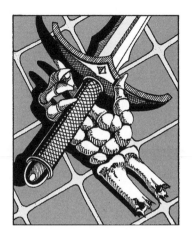

TWENTY

The sword fell to the floor, still clutched in the bony hand's dead grip.

The Boneman wailed, a terrible, horrid sound. He stared crazily at the stump of his wrist and fell to his knees, still shrieking.

King Olive stepped forward. There was an emotionless, cold light in his eyes. His face was hard and unmoving. "Boneman," he said softly.

The Boneman looked up and suddenly pounced forward, a dagger in his remaining hand. Olive moved away, but too late—the dagger plunged into his shoulder.

"*Suffer!*" cried the Boneman.

Olive grimaced in pain. "No—you suffer, you bag of bones!" Olive put every bit of strength, every hour of chained exercise, and three years of adrenaline into the sword thrust. There was a loud *k-chuk!* sound, and the Boneman's head was suddenly separated from his body. It hit the floor with the sound of a ripe melon dropped from a height.

King Olive pushed the headless body from him. It fell to the floor and twitched slightly, awaiting instructions that would never come. The guards stood unmoving, bows and swords drawn.

Rigby and Sam looked at each other. Despite the King's victory, were they still going to die?

Olive bent down to look at the severed head. "Rigby, bring me that torch."

Keeping one eye on the guards, Rigby approached with the torch.

"Hold it down here," Olive said. He inspected the head, nodding. "He wasn't just a skeleton. Look at this. He has skin, lips, ears, everything—but his skin looks transparent. You can see right through it."

"Bizarre to an extreme," Rigby said.

"How could that have happened?" Sam asked.

Olive shrugged. "I've heard stories about fish who live in water inside caves. Because they never see light, they're transparent. The Boneman spent his life in darkness, breeding darkness, spinning his dark web. It might have been the same for him."

The guards stood motionless, ready for combat, but uncertain what to do.

Olive stood, lifting the Boneman's head by the thin white hairs at the top of the skull. "Here's your cruel leader. He was supposed to be a demon. Well, I bloody well cut his head off and he's as dead as a person can get. This was his castle. It's your castle now, if you want it. If not, you're free to leave."

The guards held their weapons tensely.

"If they charge," Rigby whispered to Sam, "don't try to kill them all, just get to those stairs."

Sam nodded. He was really hoping that the guards wouldn't charge. It would make his day if the guards didn't charge.

Suddenly one of the guards leaped forward. "You killed the master!" he screamed.

Another guard behind him struck him a hard blow to the head with the hilt of his sword. The screamer collapsed on the floor.

The second guard, who seemed to be a leader, turned to the others. "Everybody else just take it easy." He turned back. "I'm Cork. You'll have to forgive him," he said, indicating the fallen man. "Boneman's had us all so scared for so long, that . . . well, it's hard to break the habit." His lips were trembling.

"All of us were taken against our will to work for him here—and we didn't dare try leave." Cork's face lowered. "I've seen the pieces of those who tried."

Several guards still had weapons raised at the ready. "Put them away," Cork said quietly. "These men are our friends."

Sam smiled, and felt the tension vanish, the muscles unknot.

"And now, ladies and gentlemen, boys and girls," Rigby said, "let's get out of this godforsaken pit."

King Olive's wound was dressed, and after a most satisfactory meal, they were given fresh horses and more provisions than they could handle.

Many of the Boneman's soldiers had immediately left for their homelands. Others stayed and were trying to decide what to do with the castle. Cork stood alone at the castle gate to see King Olive and his friends off.

"Good luck, brothers," he said.

"How can we thank you for all your help?" asked Sam.

Cork shook his head. "It is you who deserve thanks. I

feel as though I've been let loose from the devil's grip."

"And I," said Olive, looking toward the dawn.

"Let's ride, gentlemen," said Rigby. "We've got a long trip back."

The trio moved slowly away from the dark castle, the golden sun filtering down from the morning sky.

TWENTY-ONE

"Sire? Are you listening?"

"Hmm? Oh, yes, go on with your report, Aleron."

Boonder was slumped in his throne, haggard and bleary-eyed. He had not slept well in weeks, since being told that Skeet and Hatcher had escaped the fire set by his Elite warriors, and were still alive. Lord Aleron continued with his progress report on various diplomatic and political projects, but Boonder did not hear. All he could think of was being found out, deposed, mocked, imprisoned, perhaps killed. He could not enjoy the throne and the power if they might be taken from him at any time.

" . . . all possible precautions, so that such a thing can never happen again," concluded Lord Aleron. He looked up from his papers. "That's all, Your Majesty."

Boonder sighed heavily. "Very good, very good. You seem to have a good grip on things, Aleron."

"I merely serve my king as best I can."

Boonder nodded. "Yes. Well, you may go, Aleron."

"As you wish," and Lord Aleron left.

He had been gone only a minute before the door opened again; it was Captain Sarbak.

Boonder sat forward in his throne. "You have news?"

Sarbak wiped his nose. "Well, we've been following the trail of the fugitives as best we can, but it's been weeks since they started out."

"You still haven't found them?"

Sarbak laughed. "Not with the lead they've got. No, it

seems we've lost the trail."

Boonder was on his feet. *"You what!"*

"Your Majesty, that trail is weeks old, and they switched between the main road and the woods. No one could find it now. We were lucky to trace them as far as we did."

Bonder hit the back of his throne with his fist. "Don't I pay you Elite bunglers enough? Perhaps you'd understand punishment better!"

Captain Sarbak's eyes grew dark, but he said nothing.

Boonder stood still for a moment, then sank back into his throne. "Is there anything that you did discover?"

"Just that they were heading north."

Toward the Boneman, Boonder thought to himself. "You don't have any better idea where they were heading?" he asked.

Sarbak shook his head. "Just north."

King Boonder lowered his head. "That's all, Captain Sarbak. Keep me posted."

*   *   *

It was evening when the queen paid her nightly visit to the king.

"You again," Boonder said in disgust. "Why don't you leave me alone?"

Melinda smiled. Since Boonder had heard the news that Rigby and Sam were alive, he had left her totally alone. She and Boonder had separate bedrooms, ate separate meals, and really never had to see each other at all.

Except when she felt like deliberately antagonizing him.

"The worm farm in the basement has been sadly neglected lately," she said. "Don't you think you should feed the slimy little fellows?"

"I have other things on my mind!" Boonder snapped. And indeed he did, for he did not even notice how beautiful the queen was—her long auburn tresses falling softly around her shoulders, her face soft and perfect, her eyes as blue as the sea.

"Wasn't dinner good, though?" Melinda said. "The salad was fresh and crisp, the meat was tender . . . "

King Boonder closed his eyes tiredly. "Leave me, wench."

Melinda moved closer to him. "Then let me leave you forever. You have no love for me, set me free!"

Boonder looked up. "You know I will not tolerate that kind of talk." He picked up the golden worm and began stroking it feverishly. "You will respect me, my queen, for I rule this country! I am the king!"

"ARE YOU, MY BROTHER?"

The golden worm fell to the floor and shattered.

Boonder felt his heart stop. Eyes wide, he turned to face the voice. "Olive!" he choked.

"Yes," said King Olive, flanked by Rigby and Sam. All three carried drawn swords. "You don't look very happy to see me, Boonder."

"It's not possible," said Boonder weakly.

THE KING

THE BOY

THE ODDBALL

THE NOTE

THE MAIDEN

THE SORCERER

THE BONEMAN

THE ESCAPE

PART 9   THE RETURN

TWENTY-TWO

"Let my friends introduce themselves," said King Olive.

Rigby stepped forward. "I'm Rigby Skeet, rogue and sword for hire. And this is my able assistant."

Sam nodded. "Sam Hatcher. Uh . . . rogue in training."

Rigby smiled. "And we're pleased as punch to meet you."

"How did you get in here?" Boonder asked, his voice almost inaudible. "I have doubled the guards . . ."

"I know the secret passageways of this castle much better than you, my brother" Olive said. He paused for a moment and then took a step toward Boonder. "Do you know how long I rotted in that cell?"

Another step.

"Three years and eleven months. All that time, nothing but darkness. No light, just darkness."

Another step.

Melinda watched in fascination. Before her were her saviors, Hatcher and Skeet, and now King Olive himself, alive! Perhaps she could be freed from Boonder yet.

King Olive's gaze was fixed on Boonder. "I never did determine exactly what it was they were feeding me," he said. "It was the sort of filth I would never even touch with my hand, but I ate it." He laughed quietly. "And it wasn't enough." His voice rose in anger. "Sometimes I felt like crying, 'please, sir, send down more rat droppings, I'm hungry!'"

Another step. Boonder began to quiver.

"I guess I almost lost my mind. Nothing to do, and no one to talk to. I really can't imagine anything worse. Can you, brother?"

Another step.

"You want to know what kept me going all that time, all those years? It was the hope—the crazy, insane, impossible hope—that somehow I would get out. And then I would come for you, dear brother."

Another step. Perhaps only ten feet separated them now.

Melinda, still standing next to Boonder, looked at her husband. He was visibly turning into jelly.

"You're going to kill me," Boonder gasped.

"No," Olive said. "I want you to live. I want you to stand trial and then be sent to prison. I want you to rot there until you die."

Another step.

Boonder suddenly grabbed Melinda. "Don't make another move or I'll kill her!" Pulling a knife from his robe, he held it to the queen's throat.

"What the devil is he talking about?" Rigby asked. "Hey, Your Royal Lowness, she's your wife, not ours!"

"I don't care!" Boonder shrieked. "If anybody moves, I'll kill her!"

Melinda felt the cold steel against her throat. She tried very hard not to move.

King Olive shook his head, grinning. "Be serious, Boonder. Even you wouldn't murder your own wife."

"Drop your weapons or she's dead!" Boonder's eyes

were wild, blazing.

"This is ridiculous," Rigby said. "Let's charge him."

"No," Sam spoke.

Rigby turned. "Sam, what do you—"

"He'll do it," Sam said tensely. "Look at her. Look at *him*. He'll kill her, all right."

King Olive turned to Sam and looked at him coldly. "Any wench who marries my traitorous brother deserves what she gets. I'm going after Boonder."

Melinda tried to speak, to choke out a word, but she couldn't. It was as if the knife at her throat had struck her dumb.

"Begging Your Majesty's pardon," said Sam harshly, "but if you move toward Boonder, I'll kill you."

Rigby rubbed his head. "Oh boy."

Olive looked at Sam with anger in his eyes. "You saved my life, boy, but if you force me to, I swear I'll take yours."

"The girl is innocent," Sam said slowly. "And I didn't set out on this fiasco to have it end with the slaughter of innocent women."

There was a long pause.

No one moved.

The silence was absolute. And then—

King Olive slowly stepped away from Boonder and rejoined Sam and Rigby. He then dropped his sword to the ground. Sam's sword followed.

Rigby grunted. "I'm not going to like this," he said, dropping his as well.

"Good," said Boonder, still holding Melinda by the

throat. He moved slightly to one side, reaching for a rope that hung from the ceiling.

"There," he said, satisfaction replacing the fear on his face. "My Elite guards will soon enter through that door. There are ten of them, they're very skilled, and they shall kill all three of you with ease."

"Well, I'm not going to stand here and be insulted," said Rigby. "We're not welcome here, Sam, let's leave."

"Let that be your last joke, Skeet," said Boonder. He then turned to Olive. "You see, my brother, I win in the end. No matter what, I am the ultimate winner."

King Olive said nothing.

Rigby thought about all the exotic dancing girls he would never meet, all the taverns he would never be thrown out of . . .

Sam looked away from his friends, suddenly wondering if he had been wrong in his demand. What did he know about that girl? And yet, he knew if it were to happen again, his actions would be the same.

The door opened. Lord Aleron entered and closed the door behind him.

Boonder straightened. "Aleron, what are you . . ."

He suddenly stiffened and put a hand to his chest. His face was blank and his grip on Melinda relaxed. She pulled away from him.

Boonder staggered forward. "I . . . I want my worms," he gasped. Then his body seemed to lose all support and fell to the floor like a sack of potatoes. The crown slid off his greasy head and rolled away.

All eyes turned back to Lord Aleron, who was holding a long, thin wooden tube. "Blowdarts," he explained. "Tipped in the venom of the shumma snake. Brings death quite quickly."

Olive stepped forward. "Aleron, thank God you came. Boonder was crazy."

Lord Aleron nodded. "Yes. Taking a woman as hostage . . ." He shook his head. "It's not a pretty business."

Olive looked at the crumbled heap that was his brother. "He is dead?"

"Quite dead," Aleron assured him. "Who are your friends?"

"Rigby Skeet and Sam Hatcher," Olive explained. "They freed me from the cell far to the north where Boonder imprisoned me." Then he smiled broadly. "It is good to see a loyal face again, my friend." He stepped forward to embrace Lord Aleron.

"Get back!" Aleron hissed, raising the blowgun.

Olive halted, his face twisting in disbelief.

TWENTY-THREE

"I'm truly sorry, my Liege," said Lord Aleron. He turned to open the door. In came ten burly men dressed in black—the King's Elite led by Captain Sarbak.

"I'll take the one on the left," Rigby said.

Sam nodded grimly. "I'll take the rest of them."

Rigby looked doubtful. "Are you sure you can do that? Why don't I take the *two* on the left."

Sam shook his head. "No, that's okay, I can handle it."

Rigby swallowed. "If you say so."

"You see," Lord Aleron said to Olive with a sigh, "your brother was a buffoon."

King Olive's face was hard with anger. He had been betrayed again. "Tell me something I don't know."

Aleron nodded. "King Boonder was not a king. He was a man who liked to dress up and sit on a throne and eat fancy food and put worms on his slimy head. He assumed none of the duties of a king."

"You did, I take it," said Olive.

"Yes. I governed Parmall, from every minor court squabble to major diplomatic disputes. I did the leg work, the head work, everything for the past four years. Boonder just took the credit. And of course, the King's Elite I drafted for him knew from the start who their real leader was. It wasn't hard for me to convince them to betray him."

"Hey," Sam whispered to Rigby, "where's the girl?"

"Must've snuck out the back way," Rigby replied with a frown. "Lucky for her."

Olive rubbed his head tiredly. "I suppose, Aleron, that now you have some wonderful plan."

Aleron smiled. "As a matter of fact, I do. I carefully planned my takeover, waiting only for the right moment. Finally that moment is here. King Boonder declared Rigby Skeet and Sam Hatcher treacherous assassins to be killed on sight. Tonight, those two evildoers entered King Boonder's chambers and killed him. I then entered, and single-handedly killed them both." He paused. "I shall be made king within a week."

"And I?" said King Olive coldly.

"I'm afraid your body will not be found, my king. After all, you died almost four years ago." Lord Aleron lowered his head slightly. "I am truly sorry that things had to turn out this way."

Olive spat, hitting Aleron squarely in the eye, and smiled. "It's my one new skill," he said. "There was nothing else to do in that cell."

Reaching for his handkerchief, Lord Aleron scowled and turned to the King's Elite. "Captain Sarbak . . ."

"King Olive, here!" cried Rigby suddenly. "Your sword!"

Olive ran to join Sam and Rigby. The three men held their swords tightly.

"Kill them all," Aleron instructed. "Try to make Skeet and Hatcher a clean job—not too much hacking around the edges. Something I could have done by myself. As for King Olive . . . " Aleron finished wiping his eye. "Do with him as you like."

The killers in black moved forward.

"Wait," said Rigby, pushing Olive aside and stepping forward. "Aleron, if you and your men surrender now, I promise we will let you live."

The King's Elite guards paused. Aleron looked up with contempt. "Rigby Skeet, you're insane."

Rigby grinned. "I know you are, but what am I?"

"I have no time for this nonsense," Aleron growled. "Sarbak . . ."

"Think about it. Could a crazy man storm the castle of the Boneman and bring back King Olive?" Rigby asked. "Oh, and by the way, the Boneman had at least twenty guards, not just a measly ten."

"Rigby Skeet," Aleron sighed, "I try to take pity on women, children, and morons, but you must die, and all your babbling will not save you. Captain Sarbak . . ."

Rigby whirled. "All right, Sam! On my signal, *kill them!*"

Sam looked incredulous. "All of them?"

"Yes, all of them!" Rigby snapped.

Sam gritted his teeth, then nodded. One of the Elite guards looked toward Sarbak. "Sir, maybe we ought to wait or something . . ."

"Enough nonsense!" Lord Aleron cried. "Captain Sarbak, attack!"

The ten ugly brutes moved in on their prey.

"Well, it was a nice bluff, Rigby," said Sam. "At least you bought us some time."

"What bluff?" said Rigby, his face calm. "Let's kill 'em."

"Yes," said King Olive, torn by anger and anguish. "Let's."

Suddenly the door flew open.

And in poured fighting men, dressed in bold green—the green of the Royal Guard!

Captain Clerret, old but tough, led the fray. "For King Olive!" he cried. "And justice!"

The thugs in black had begun to attack Olive and his rescuers, but now their ranks were thrown into confusion. Rigby had already cut one man down and was dueling with another when a Royal Guardsman came to his aid, bashing the Elite warrior's head from behind.

"Rats, I wanted to do that," gasped Rigby, "But thanks."

Sam and the king were holding their own, but now the entrance of the Royal Guardsmen had set the odds firmly in their favor. The King's Elite were really only thugs and brigands dressed as warriors, and they had none of the training and precision of the Royal Guard.

One of the King's Elite lunged at Sam with his sword. "Die, swine!" he howled.

Sam threw a lit candle at his face, sidestepped the thrust, and kicked the brute in the stomach. Hard. The attacker stumbled backward and collapsed on the floor.

"No rules in a sword fight," Sam reminded his unconscious foe.

*   *   *

Captain Sarbak stood to one side. His men were dropping like flies! How could this be happening? How could the plan have failed? Why was there a sword at his neck?

"Hi, there," said Rigby. "Care to drop your weapons, or

do you prefer instant death?"

Captain Sarbak's weapons fell to the ground—It was not his day.

"Aleron!" yelled King Olive, as he fought his way across the room.

Lord Aleron turned pale. He tried to move away, but not fast enough. Breathing hard, he drew his sword.

Olive looked at the sword and grinned. "I thought you'd stolen my revenge, Aleron. But maybe not."

Olive lunged, and Aleron's sword clattered to the floor.

Aleron stared at his empty hands in disbelief. Then he hurriedly reached into a pocket and brought forth the deadly blowgun. Olive's sword flashed forward again, and the blowgun lay in pieces on the floor.

"Rats, I wanted to do that," said Rigby, watching from across the room.

Lord Aleron panicked and raced to the window, his only avenue of escape. As King Olive rushed after him, Aleron lost his footing on the windowsill. His terrified screams echoed into the room as he fell hundreds of feet to his death.

*   *   *

The battle ended rather swiftly. Almost all of the blood, gore, and severed ears belonged to the King's Elite.

King Olive sheathed his sword. "It's over. I am king once more." There were long gashes along his face and chest, but he seemed not to feel them.

"And we are glad to have you back, Sire," said Captain Clerret.

Olive smiled. "I owe you my life, you old scoundrel." He turned to Rigby and Sam. "And you, Rigby Skeet and Sam Hatcher, I owe you my life and my freedom. How can I repay you?"

Rigby grinned. "I'm sure we'll be able to work something out. I'm thinking boundless treasure, infinite power— you know, stuff like that."

But Sam's mind was elsewhere. "How did the Royal Guard know we were here? Who sent them?"

"I did," said a soft, melodious voice.

Sam looked up into the most beautiful face he had ever seen. "You're Boonder's wife."

Melinda shook her head. "I was his slave. He forced me to marry him against my will." She sighed. "And you were right. He would have killed me, but you saved me." And with that, she walked up to Sam and kissed him lightly on the lips.

Sam got the kind of stunned look that a man gets when he's just been punched in the stomach. After the initial shock, he looked at her with what could only be called love in his eyes.

"I don't even know your name," Sam said softly.

"Melinda," she said, and this time, Sam kissed *her*.

"Rats, I wanted to do that," said Rigby.

EPILOGUE

Sam and Melinda were married two weeks later.

King Olive insisted that the wedding take place in the Royal Hall, a vast structure normally reserved for official functions. As the ceremony began, members of the Royal Guard led the procession, with Captain Clerret at the front. Alongside was Sam's father, Milos, wearing his Royal Guard uniform for the first time in twenty years. Rigby walked in step a few feet behind, and winked at Sam as he walked by.

Sam beamed when he saw Milos, proud that he had lived up to his father's dreams, as well as his own. He looked at his mother, sitting in the front of this regal hall with its high, arched ceiling, and saw her tears of joy. And then he saw Melinda. She wore a simple, elegant white gown.

Sam had never seen a girl so beautiful in all his life.

The ceremony was much more tasteful than Melinda's first wedding. King Olive assisted the palace priest with the wedding rites, including the reading of the forty Holy Orders. The next thing Sam knew, he was kissing the bride.

And liking it very much.

*   *   *

After a beautiful honeymoon near the Sands of White Cliff, Sam and Melinda found a small cottage near the village square, and bought it with part of the "thank-you" money King Olive had given them. Shortly after that, Sam joined with Rigby, with the two partners operating as *Skeet*

& Hatcher, Swords for Hire.

With a little help from twelve members of the King's staff, and the entire Royal Guard unit, they built a log house where Rigby's shack had stood. The new headquarters of Skeet & Hatcher was a vast improvement, with an open living area and kitchen at the front, and Rigby's bedroom in back. Of course, Rigby insisted that the original tunnel be reopened and cleared of debris.

"Hey, if you recall, that tunnel did save our lives," Rigby reminded Sam.

Their daily routine was straightforward. After breakfast at their cottage, Sam and Melinda would walk the short distance to their headquarters, where the three would spend the day. Sam and Melinda took turns helping Rigby learn to read, and after several months, he had finally advanced from children's books. He sat at the table, slowly working his way through his first "real" book, a fat adventure tale by S. Morgenstern.

"Why don't they have books where someone's taken out all the extra stuff, and just kept the good parts?" asked Rigby. "This thing is killing me."

"Sorry, that's not the way it works," said Melinda, who was standing with Sam as they prepared the day's lunch.

"Yeah, thanks. And I suppose you think you can make me eat my broccoli, too," Rigby replied. "Not bloody likely, missy!"

"Sam, where on earth did you find this uncouth, unpredictable man?" joked Melinda.

After a brief pause, Sam said, "Uh, right here."

Even though each had learned new skills, Melinda was beginning to grow restless. It had been over six months since they had formed Skeet & Hatcher, and they had yet to embark on even the smallest task.

True, they had appeared at the King's Autumn Festival and at the Golden Ceremony for the bicentennial of the kingdom. Both times the crowd's praise had been deafening as they cheered the heroes who had saved the king's life.

But Melinda didn't understand how Sam and Rigby could spend each and every day reading, practicing their fencing skills, sharpening swords and knives, and exercising on their crude obstacle course. Again and again and again.

She pulled a loaf of coarse-grain bread from the oven, set it on the oak table, then looked at Rigby and Sam.

"Is this what we're going to do?" she asked. "Surely we should have had something by now? I'm sorry, but I'm just getting tired of the same thing, day after day."

"Well, here's the thing," said Rigby. "Adventure doesn't schedule well—it just happens when it happens. I think I read that in my book."

"But that's just it!" snapped Melinda. "We've been here half a year, and *nothing* has happened, nothing at all. I love you, Sam, and I thought I could live like this, but . . . maybe I can't."

Sam calmly watched Melinda, but was silent.

Rigby grinned, then finally said, "I promise—cross my heart—we'll have exciting adventures where we can risk our lives and maybe even get killed."

Melinda smiled weakly. "But when?"

"Has anyone ever told you you're weird?" said Rigby.

Sam finally spoke. "Melinda, trust me. It's been pretty slow lately, but you never know when duty may call."

At that instant, a man with three arrows in his body staggered in through the open doorway, gasped, and fell to the floor.

Melinda's eyes and mouth opened wide. She stared at the man on the floor, then looked in astonishment at Rigby.

Rigby's eyes shifted back and forth. He opened his mouth as if to speak, then finally looked toward Sam.

Sam turned to Melinda, smiled, and said simply, "So . . . now are you happy?"

*   *   *

Over the years, Sam and Rigby went off together on many bold missions and quests. And although she was firmly told to stay at home, Melinda accompanied them more often than not. The Swords for Hire team fought the Hordes of Mintar, and the Giant of Hoogan, and the Great Mingus Dragon, and . . .

And they lived rather hectically ever after.

Swords For Hire

ABOUT THE AUTHOR

Almost from the day he was born, Will Allen was a writer.

Growing up in Kettering, Ohio, he wrote anything and everything—literally hundreds of songs, poems, and stories, as well as dozens of short movies filmed on an 8mm film camera in those days before VCRs and camcorders. At Ohio University in the late 1970s, he conceived *Campus*, a comedy radio show, and personally wrote and directed each of the 102 episodes.

Swords for Hire was inspired by William Goldman's *The Princess Bride*, one of Will's favorite books by one of Will's favorite authors. Other favorites included Stephen King, Ray Bradbury, Robert Heinlein, and Mark Twain.

Will was diagnosed with melanoma, a form of cancer, in the spring of 1978. He fought the disease for two years, but ultimately the disease won. Will wrote *Swords for Hire* in the fall of 1979, giving copies to family members and close friends on Christmas day. He died exactly four months later, just a few weeks before his twenty-third birthday.

*   *   *   *   *

Please forward comments to Will's brother, Paul, in care of the publisher or at: info@centerpunchpress.com

ABOUT THIS EDITION

Comments from the author's brother

I loved *Swords for Hire* when Will gave it to us over twenty years ago, and I've read it many times since, but I had never thought about publishing it. Then a year or so ago, I read it aloud to my daughters, and as I spoke, the story and characters really came to life for me. It was then I realized that *Swords for Hire* might have a future much bigger than its original four or five copies.

Of course, my daughters loved it, and they were excited that their Uncle Will, who had died over ten years before they were born, had written it. But the real measure was the overwhelming reaction from some of my book-loving friends. After I distributed several copies, almost every comment was a superlative. People quoted their favorite parts or lines of dialogue. Everyone, young or old, loved the story and the characters—even the greasy-haired, worm-loving bad guy.

As a result of this universally-enthusiastic response, I began this project by typing the story into my Mac. This gave me a new appreciation for how hard Will worked, writing and typing on an typewriter while he was ill. I spent many months reading and rereading it, until I had the story almost memorized. I edited a few sections slightly, but what you read here is 100% Will's story.

Swords for Hire proved itself when a preliminary printing won a national award in a contest held by *Writer's Digest Magazine*. The results were announced in their August 2002 issue, twenty-two years after the story was written. I think Will would be as proud of his story as I am.

Will's widow, Annie, has reviewed this edition and helped keep me on target with my work. Annie is married to a great guy, Steve, and their boys, Evan and Connor, are also big fans of *Swords for Hire*.

In keeping with the book's fun theme, I decided to have real people represent the characters on the cover. A good friend recommended science fiction and fantasy illustrator David Michael Beck, well-known for his work with Wildstorm, Chaos, Image and Marvel comics, G.I. Joe, and the Everquest computer game.

I took him some old photos, then had a longtime family friend, Dave "Dēt" Dietrichson, pose as King Olive. On the resulting cover painting, the "good guy" characters, from left to right, are: Will as Sam Hatcher, Paul as Rigby, Dēt as King Olive, and Annie as Melinda. (Of course, Boonder and the Boneman are *not* based on real people.)

I hope you enjoy Will's book.

Paul Allen

ACKNOWLEDGMENTS

Thanks to my daughters, Marcy, Lisa, and Stephanie, and to Annie's sons, Evan and Connor, for reminding me how good *Swords for Hire* really is.

Thanks to Beth Andrews for continuously nudging me toward completion of this project.

Thanks to April Kerley for her enthusiasm and for telling me about the Writer's Digest book competition.

Thanks to Laurie Ann Devereaux, Sandi Kline, and Deb Dietrichson for proofreading, and special thanks to Nicole Bentley for her expert help in polishing the final version. (I didn't always follow these folks' advice, so any errors in the book are of my own doing.)

Thanks to Dave Wendt, for his Photoshop expertise, and for introducing me to . . .

Dave Beck, who I thank for the incredible job on the illustrations throughout the book and the wonderful cover painting.

Thanks to Bob Dilgard for the great cover design.

Thanks to Annie Strand, Will's widow, for encouraging this project and reviewing my editing.

Thanks to my wife, Brenda, for putting up with me as I spent my evenings on my Mac, whether I was working on this project or looking for vintage neon signs on eBay!

Special thanks to Nancy Cartwright for sharing her memories of Will in the foreword.

And most of all, thanks to Will, for being a great brother—sorry about chasing you around the yard with my go-cart—and for leaving us so much of yourself in your incredible writing, with *Swords for Hire* being only one example.

Paul Allen